LET ME HOLD YOU

This Large Print Book carries the
Seal of Approval of N.A.V.H.

LET ME HOLD YOU

MELANIE SCHUSTER

THORNDIKE PRESS

A part of Gale, Cengage Learning

GALE
CENGAGE Learning·

Farmington Hills, Mich • San Francisco • New York • Waterville, Maine
Meriden, Conn • Mason, Ohio • Chicago

GALE
CENGAGE Learning·

LIBRARY OF CONGRESS CATALOGING-IN-PUBLICATION DATA

Schuster, Melanie, 1951–
    Let me hold you / by Melanie Schuster. — Large Print edition.
        pages cm. — (Thorndike Press Large Print African-American)
    ISBN 978-1-4104-6747-8 (hardcover) — ISBN 1-4104-6747-3 (hardcover)
    1. African Americans—Fiction. 2. Large type books. I. Title.
PS3619.C48328L48 2014
813'.6—dc23   2013047778

Published in 2014 by arrangement with Harlequin Books S.A.

Printed in Mexico
1 2 3 4 5 6 7 18 17 16 15 14

This is dedicated with sincere appreciation to my editor, Tracy Sherrod, for her encouragement, her expertise and above all, her patience. She put up with a lot during the creation of this book and I thank her from the bottom of my heart. Her support meant the world to me.

To my readers, who as always support me and encourage me. It always means a lot to me, but even more when I was down for the count!

Thanks also to Dr. Minoo Khetarpal and Dr. Gavin Awerbuch for getting me well.

And a special thanks to Pam and Joyce for all your help; I never would have made it without you!

CHAPTER 1

"This is the best party I've been to since you got married," Alana Sharp Dumond announced. She raised her flute of champagne to her sister, Alexis Sharp VanBuren. Alexis had married her true love, Jared VanBuren, in a fabulous Valentine's Day wedding and now, the Saturday before Christmas, they were at the reception of Sherri Stratton and Lucas VanBuren, Jared's younger brother.

Alexis took a sip of her alcohol-free spumante and smiled at her older sister. She wasn't drinking because she and Jared were expecting their first baby. "We started off the year with a wedding and we're ending it with one. Perfect symmetry, I'd say."

"A great way to end the year," Alana agreed. "Yes, I'd love some more," she added happily to the waiter who was offering to refill her glass.

Alexis raised a carefully groomed eyebrow as Alana took a rather healthy swallow of her drink. "You better slow down, sister. You've had quite a bit of that tonight."

Alana grinned to show that she didn't take offense at her younger sister's words of caution. "I'm drinking for two since you can't have any. Don't worry, I'm fine. I've eaten enough food for two linebackers and it's soaking up all the alcohol very nicely. Now I want to dance," she said cheerfully.

They were sitting at the long table set up for the wedding party, which was being held at Seven-Seventeen, the stylish and successful upscale restaurant owned by the Van-Buren brothers and their friend, Roland Casey. The VanBurens were chefs and restaurateurs and Roland was their partner. The table was mostly empty at the moment, since the bride and groom were out on the dance floor looking at each other with the eyes of love. Jared and Roland were outside smoking expensive cigars while most of the other attendants were either dancing or taking funny pictures in the photo booth that had been rented for the occasion.

Alana could sense Alexis getting ready to continue the conversation about her intake of Moet and she beckoned to David Stratton, Sherri's brother.

"C'mon and dance with me, David," she said. "We haven't had a chance to catch up

10

yet." Giving her sister a wink, she took his hand and they went to join the other dancers just as the music changed to something fast and jazzy.

Alexis sighed while she watched the two of them head for the dance floor. Alana was just a bit too giddy for her taste, not that her older sister would act up or make a scene. It just wasn't like her to imbibe so much, but it was such a festive occasion that who could blame her?

Jared and Roland came back to the table looking rakish and debonair in their tuxedoes with the ties loosened. Her husband sat down and pulled her chair close to his side before putting his arm around her and kissing her neck, enjoying the little purr that she always made when he did that.

Roland grinned at the two of them and said, "Get a room, you two. Where's my beautiful partner?" He scanned the room looking for Alana, with whom he'd been paired in the wedding.

Alexis stroked her husband's face and sighed as he took her hand and kissed the palm. "She's out on the dance floor shaking her booty," she replied.

Roland made a face of mock outrage as his eyes found Alana, who was indeed dancing in a lively but sexy fashion with David

Stratton. "I'll see you two scandalous people later. I'm going to reclaim my woman-to-be," he announced as he took off in her direction.

Alexis laughed softly as Jared pulled her out of her chair and into his lap. "What's that about?" she murmured.

"Roland likes Alana," he answered. "He says she's been dodging him long enough and he's about to stake his claim."

"I wish him luck with that one," Alexis said dryly. "Bolder men than Roland have tried to storm Fort Alana and failed. They all come home bruised and empty-handed."

Jared was busy kissing the back of her hand but he stopped long enough to answer her. "You don't know Roland. My family always called him my brother from another mother because we're alike in so many ways. Number one, we know our woman when we see her. And number two, the word *no* means 'try harder' to us. We don't give up when we really want something and I have a feeling that Roland really wants Alana."

"I wish him luck, but he's got his work cut out for him. In the meantime, I want to go be sociable with our folks and then go home. I need some alone time with my baby before our baby gets here," she said with a teasing light in her eyes.

Alana was just leaving the dance floor when a strong arm went around her waist. She looked up in surprise and then she smiled at Roland.

"I take it you want to dance," she said teasingly.

"I do. You're supposed to be my partner and I've been deprived of your company for too long," he replied.

"Well, we'll have to make up for lost time, then."

The music was a slow number and Roland was a great dancer. He'd taken off his tuxedo jacket and the way his broad shoulders looked in his shirt was amazing. As he held her close, she could detect the sexy scent of a rich, expensive cigar and equally pricy cognac. Before she could stop herself she leaned in closer and took a deep sniff and detected the even more enticing scent of his skin. She felt his muscular chest move as he laughed softly.

"Find anything you like?" he asked. His voice was deep, sensual and even headier than his fragrance.

"You smell good," she answered. "Really, really good. You're a good dancer, too."

She raised her eyes to his and studied him carefully. It was almost like seeing him for the first time, which was crazy. She'd met Roland months ago after he and Lucas Van-Buren had moved from Chicago to Columbia to open Seven-Seventeen. They'd been around each other quite a bit, at family gatherings and the like, but she couldn't claim to know him very well, no better than he knew her. Gazing at him now, she took in every one of his features and realized that they added up to a very compelling package.

Roland was tall, maybe even taller than Jared. He was much more muscular than Jared, though; he was built like a linebacker. His skin was a rich deep brown with red undertones, smooth as milk chocolate. His eyes were penetrating, with thick black eyebrows and lashes that were way too long and pretty for a man. With his high cheekbones and chiseled lips, he could have been almost feminine except for his strong, slightly hooked nose and his neatly trimmed goatee. His head was bald and perfectly shaped and all in all, he was an extremely handsome man.

"Is there something on my face? Spinach in my teeth?" Roland looked amused instead of put off, which was good.

"I've been staring at you, haven't I? Sorry about that," Alana said with a crooked smile. "I usually have better manners than this."

"It's quite all right with me, I liked it. This is the longest you've looked at me since we met. Did you like what you see? I mean, do I pass?"

"You get an A-plus," she replied. "An A-plus-plus, as a matter of fact."

Roland's eyes lit up and his smile was warm enough to melt a glacier. "Now we're getting somewhere," he said. His voice was so silky and deep it was like having a Pashmina draped over her bare shoulders.

There was something so oddly familiar about being in his arms that Alana was at a loss for words, something that no one close to her had ever witnessed. Alana always had a comeback, usually something smart and snappy. But tonight she just enjoyed the feeling of Roland's arms around her and his body next to hers as they moved to the sultry music. They had three dances and when the jazz trio took a break they drifted off the floor with their hands locked together. It was as if neither of them could think of a good reason to let go, so they didn't. They stayed together for the rest of the reception.

Roland was pleased with the new turn of events. He'd been unable to stop staring at Alana all day. It was the first time in weeks that he'd been able to spend any significant time with her and he meant to take full advantage of every minute. Alana Sharp Dumond was an elusive, mysterious beauty that he wanted to get to know better and as soon as possible.

She'd looked gorgeous during the ceremony in the strapless gold brocade and chiffon dresses worn by the bridesmaids, but she looked even better at the reception. The dresses had an overskirt that his sisters informed him was a peplum with a demi-train, which was removed after the ceremony for dancing. Now he could see her beautiful long legs.

It was easy to figure out that the Sharp women were sisters; Alana, Adrienne, Alexis and Ava were all chocolate beauties with shining black hair, beautiful skin and petite figures. When his best friend, Jared, had introduced him to Alexis the first time, Roland had immediately asked if she had any sisters at home. When Jared got finished laughing at the remark, he told Roland that she had a houseful of them and he could have his pick. But when he'd met Alana, he'd known that he wasn't looking any further. Alana wasn't making things easy for him, however.

Whenever he saw her in a crowd of people, she was warm and friendly, full of humorous conversation and borderline flirtatious. How she was in a one-on-one situation he didn't know because she was a master of avoidance. He'd asked her out a few times and she always managed to have some ironclad reason not to go. Normally he would've moved on and found a more willing companion without giving her a second thought. He was far from conceited but he wasn't unaware that he had a certain magnetism when it came to women. He was the oldest of seven children; there were five younger sisters between him and the youngest, his brother, Glenn.

He'd spent his adolescence ducking and dodging the myriad of besotted friends of his sisters, all of whom wanted him for their very own. It was something of a relief to him when he went off to college so he hadn't had to worry about hurting some young girl's feelings. One thing he wasn't used to was being ignored, though, and Alana's behavior was close to a total shutout. Normally he would have returned the favor and gone on his merry way, but there was something about her that captivated him.

He was having a great time with her, going from table to table talking to family and friends. His family had come down from Chicago for the festivities, as they had been close to the VanBurens since Jared and Roland were small boys. Alana and his sisters had hit it off when Jared and Alexis got married and they were gossiping like sorority sisters while Roland had a chance to look at Alana as much as he liked.

Her glossy black hair was twisted into some kind of updo that showed off her long slender neck and drew attention to her oval face with the big almond-shaped eyes. Her features were delicate but sensual, especially her lips. They were a perfect cupid's bow, but plump and inviting like a ripe plum. Everything about her was fine and elegant, from her slender shoulders and arms to her long, artistic fingers. It was hard to believe that she was a mechanic, but she owned Custom Classics, the top auto repair and custom paint shop in Columbia. Her business was the best place in South Carolina to get a car restored to its former glory, especially if it was a vintage model. She even had offers for reality TV; producers were constantly after her to make a series about her business but she turned them all down.

He would have been content to watch her for hours, but his youngest sister, Pamela, chose to tease him about his fascination. She'd taken a vacant chair next to him and started meddling, which was one of her favorite things to do.

"Your eyes are gonna fall out if you don't stop looking. I think you're drooling, do you want a bib?" Her eyes were full of merriment, but her lips were barely moving, a trick she'd mastered years ago when she wanted to talk in church, in class or anywhere else she was supposed to be quiet.

"Quiet, you nosy wench," Roland said with an unmistakable note of fondness in his voice. He loved his sisters madly even though their sole purpose in life seemed to be to get on his last good nerve. "Go find yourself something else to do besides get in my business or my retaliation will be both painful and public."

Pamela grinned wickedly as she glanced with great interest from Alana to her big brother. "You need to take a picture, it'll last longer."

"That's original. Never heard that one before," Roland muttered as he gazed at the delectable nape of Alana's neck.

"I mean it," protested Pamela. "There's a

photo booth over there. You should get this moment commemorated because it might be the closest you get to her for the rest of your life." She yelped as Roland thumped her on the back of her head.

He did follow through with her suggestion, though. After Alana took her last sip of champagne they went over to the booth and found it empty. They attempted to sit on the bench but his long legs took up most of the room so she sat on his lap. Her perfume was as sweet and captivating as she was and as she closed the curtain he inhaled the fragrant essence that was one part Chanel No. 5 and three parts Alana.

The camera clicked as they smiled into the lens and made funny faces. She closed her eyes and planted a big smacking kiss on his cheek, which he returned. Their eyes met and by an unspoken mutual consent their lips touched softly and deliberately before merging into a powerful kiss. Roland was right; her lips were like fragrant plums dipped in champagne and the taste released a powerful longing in him. Their tongues mated and lingered, stoking the growing fire between them.

Alana's arms went around his neck and he pulled her closer to him, crushing her soft breasts against his rock-hard chest. His hands slid down to her slim hips and she pressed against him harder as one slim hand stroked his smoothly shaven head. It could have gone on and on but the curtain was suddenly pushed aside by two smirking women, Pamela and Ava.

"I told you they were in here," Pamela gloated.

"You two should probably get a room somewhere," Ava advised. "There are children and old people here, you know. You could give somebody a heart attack."

"I should have known you would find each other," Alana said with a resigned expression. "Aren't there some interesting men out there for you to torture?"

Pamela grinned and said, "Yes, there are, but this is more fun. How much will you pay me to keep these pictures off of Facebook?" She was reaching for the photo strips when Roland grabbed her wrist firmly.

"I'll let you live, how's that?" He gave her the expression that she knew meant business and since Alana was giving Ava a similar look, they decided to leave.

"We can go spread gossip, that's almost as good," Pam said pragmatically.

Roland and Alana looked at each other and burst out laughing. "Is there any lipstick on my mouth?" he asked.

Alana assured him there wasn't. "This is the non-smear, perma-shine kind. No smears, I promise."

"Well, in that case, I think we need to finish what we started," he murmured, just before his mouth joined hers for one more mindlessly sweet kiss.

CHAPTER 2

The morning after the wedding found Alana in a mood that most charitably could be described as foul. Her head was pounding from all the bubbly Moet she'd had at the reception and she wanted nothing more than to be alone for the rest of the day and possibly her life. Sitting up in her bed seemed to take all of her energy and she groaned loudly and with great pain. It was going to be a miserable day.

Only a few drinks in her system, and she could barely remember what she'd done the night before. Compounding that was the fact that she'd had an array of dreams that were blazingly hot, featuring Roland Casey as her partner in every kind of erotic crime imaginable. Why in the world she'd managed to conjure the two of them, naked, sweaty and tightly entwined the way she had was just beyond her. There were some mental puzzle pieces missing, but her head hurt too badly for her to figure it out at the moment.

After her eyelids finally came unglued, she squinted around her bedroom, trying to figure out where her robe was. Since her sister Adrienne was staying with her, she tried to do it as quietly as possible, although it was so late that Adrienne was probably awake. Alana was in no shape to converse with anyone, however, and she was aiming for total stealth at the moment.

She managed to find the robe and her slippers and she staggered into the bathroom, hoping that a blast of hot water on her face would bring her back to the land of the living.

The shower was a mixed blessing because her head was throbbing so hard that the stream of water was actually quite painful, but she clenched her teeth and hung in there, scrubbing her body mercilessly with a nylon puff and a huge amount of Au Lait body wash.

The mild, clean scent gradually soothed her senses until she was at least able to move her neck without wincing. While she moved the puff up and down her body she tried to recreate the evening, hoping that there was a reasonable explanation for her steamy dreams and her deep sense of embarrassment. Maybe she had an alter-ego like Beyonce, she thought mirthlessly. Maybe her personal Sasha Fierce had taken over her dreams last night because it sure wasn't the real Alana. With a sigh that came from the depths of her being, she turned the water off and stepped out of the shower, wrapping herself in a big soft towel before putting the robe on again.

Adrienne was probably up and moving around because the thermostat had been turned up and the house was no longer chilly. She could also smell her favorite morning aroma, coffee. God bless her, Adrienne knew the only thing that would help her headache was a large cup of joe. Maybe the whole pot.

Alana made a detour through the living room on her way to the kitchen and found her shoes, which had been left by the front door. She also found the attachment to her gown, the rest of her dress, her purse, her jewelry and everything else she'd worn that she'd apparently tossed this way and that as she'd staggered into the house. That must have been some striptease she'd done on the way to the bed.

Hauling everything into the bedroom, she was about to pile her clothes onto the window seat, but it was already occupied by

Adrienne, who was holding a large mug out to her.

"Just toss 'em on the bed, Sissie. Let's talk," Adrienne said brightly. "Sissie" was the name Adrienne had called her from the time she was first able to talk.

Alana dropped the clothes and reached for the mug, which her sister pulled away. "Not a chance, not until you agree to talk to me."

"Fine, whatever, just give me that coffee and tell me what's on your mind."

"You're on my mind, sweetie. I'm concerned about you," Adrienne said, her eyebrows raised slightly. "I thought you could use a listening ear."

Alana took another long swallow and stared into the mug like it was a Magic 8-Ball or some other kind of oracle. "Did I do something stupid last night that I don't recall?"

"No, you were actually behaving like the Alana that I've always loved and admired and tried to emulate. You've been my role model since the day I was born. We practically shared the same womb," Adrienne said with a grin.

It was true; Alana and Adrienne were born only ten months apart, and were as close as twins in a lot of ways, even physically, although Adrienne was a lot more bohemian than Alana. Alana's style tended to be more classic while her younger sister wore avant-garde garb of her own design. She was a much sought-after costume designer in Hollywood and she looked the part.

Alana's relaxed hair was worn in a sleek shoulder-length bob, while Adrienne's hair was worn in wild spiraling curls. She also wore glasses because she couldn't be bothered with contact lenses, and she always managed to find stunningly fashionable ones that showed off her eyes instead of hiding them.

The sisters were the same height and size, although Adrienne was heavier now that she was entering the second trimester of her pregnancy. She'd thought she was pregnant back in February when Alexis got married, but it had been a false alarm. This time it was the real deal. She was definitely with child, a child she was sure was a boy, even before the ultrasound had proved her to be correct.

"Why in the world would you want to be like me? I'm completely and totally boring. I think your hormones are making you a little crazy," Alana said as she put the mug on her nightstand. She picked up a bottle of Au Lait body lotion and began applying it to her legs before continuing.

"You're avoiding my question," she said sternly. "What did I do last night? I'm having a problem remembering some details, like how my clothes got strewn all over the living room."

"You didn't do anything scandalous, if that's what you mean. You were a little frisky, no doubt due to the amount of champagne you had, but all you did was dance a lot. And you took some cute pictures with Roland."

"Cute pictures? What cute pictures?" Alana demanded as she took off her robe to finish putting on lotion.

Adrienne gladly handed her the strips from the photo booth and sat back to watch her reaction. She didn't have long to wait as Alana's cheeks turned red and her eyes got huge.

"Good Lord. I forgot all about these," she mumbled. "Was I drunk or what? How did I get home? Did I make a fool out of myself?"

Adrienne laughed at the look on her sister's face. "I brought you home because Roland took his parents back to the hotel. On the way home you started singing and you kept on singing when we got to the house. Then you started dancing through the living room, tossing your clothes. It was pretty cute. Actually, you were singing 'I Want a Hippopotamus for Christmas' and it was hilarious."

Alana made a scornful noise and continued her grooming routine, putting body butter on her feet, elbows and knees. "You're just making things up to get on my nerves. I don't remember doing anything of the kind. I had a little to drink but not that much. I certainly would've remembered a performance like that," she said haughtily. Holding her towel tightly, she went into her walk-in closet and emerged wearing a lacy pink bra and matching thong.

Adrienne was waiting for her, holding out her smartphone. Alana leaned over to get a good look at it and squealed when she saw the video playing on the screen. There she was in all her giddy glory, singing loud and off-key as her clothes went flying.

"How do you delete this?" Alana turned the phone over and over, examining all the buttons. "If this ends up on your Facebook page, I'll get you," she vowed.

"I was thinking more like YouTube," Adrienne teased. "Or that funny video show on TV. We could make some money, honey."

Alana tossed the phone to her unrepentant sister and went back to the closet for jeans and a sweater. Adrienne continued to talk to her while she dressed.

"You didn't do anything really crazy last night. You were acting like a normal, happy, sexy woman. I love these photo booth pictures because they're you, the real you. I was so happy to see you dancing through the house last night without a care in the world because that's how you should be. There's nothing wrong with being with a delicious man who's obviously interested in you. I haven't seen you like this since . . ." Her voice trailed away for a moment and then she finished. "Since Sam died. You deserve to start living again, Sissie."

Alana picked up her mug and drained the rest of her coffee, which was now stone-cold and tasted like prune juice. "I'm hungry. Are you hungry? C'mon, I'll make you some breakfast," she said as she abruptly left the room.

Adrienne sighed deeply as she watched her sister depart, but in seconds she was right on her heels. She found her in the kitchen staring into the refrigerator. "I already made some scones, all you have to do is make an omelet if you feel up to it," she said hopefully.

"Sure, no problem. Are you eating meat these days or what?"

"If it's smaller than me and can't get away, I'll devour it, whatever it is. I'm gonna be as big as a house in a few weeks," Adrienne said as she rubbed her still-tiny belly.

Alana emerged from the refrigerator with eggs, cream, cheese, scallions, mushrooms and sausage. "Can you get me a red pepper and that package of bacon, please?"

"Only if you talk to me," Adrienne said, but she opened the door to get the items. "You can't shut me out because you know I'll wear you down."

Alana busied herself chopping and slicing and getting out the skillets. Her kitchen was large, orderly and well-stocked; it looked like a place where a person could get some serious cooking done. To forestall a spate of wheedling from her persistent sister, she began talking as she put the sausage on to brown.

"Look, Adrienne, there's nothing to talk about, really. Nothing much has changed around here. I'm still working hard and that's about it. If you want to talk about changes, Alexis is your girl. She's the newlywed and the expectant mother. And you've got your own little bun in the oven. Isn't that enough of a change for you?"

Adrienne reached for a piece of the bright red sweet pepper before answering. "We can

31

talk about me anytime. I want to know how you're doing. I know how hard the holidays are for you, that's why you always come out to California to stay with me, or you go to New York to stay with Aunt BeBe. But since we're both here you won't be able to hide out like you usually do. Don't you think we should talk about that?"

Alana cracked the eggs on the side of the glass bowl with amazing accuracy and a bit more force than normal. She poured in some cream and shook in salt, pepper and paprika before picking up the whisk and beating them into a fluffy froth.

It was true; Alana had a lot of difficulty with the holidays these days. Ever since her husband had died the week before Christmas, all she could think about at this time of year was losing the love of her life.

It was so unfair; it was so wrong that he'd died so young. There were times when she knew deep in her soul that she was doomed to be alone forever. No one could ever take his place in her heart or her life and that was just the way it was going to be. She'd be a lonely widow for the rest of her life and spend all her time and money doting on the nieces and nephews she was sure to accumulate.

With three younger sisters and several

sister-friends, she knew that she'd be blessed with many children in her life one way or the other. Giving herself a sharp mental kick in the head, she forced herself to focus on the here and now and to stop being neurotic. Alana had no patience with weak and whiny people, and she wasn't about to turn into one herself, especially now.

She always pretended that everything was well in her world, but it was really hard to keep up the façade in the middle of all the celebrating. Her family was big on Christmas and she just didn't have it in her to celebrate anymore. It was easier to head for sunny California and hide out with Adrienne because her younger sister understood the situation better than anyone else. But this year Adrienne was here in Columbia and she had no reason to hide out in LA. Nor could she take refuge in New York with her mother's sister who was her other haven in the storm of emotions that arose every Christmas.

She did, however, have a way of deflecting her sister's interrogation by changing the subject to Adrienne's situation, which she did.

"Do you mind setting the table for us? These will be finished in about two minutes. And I think a much better topic for us to discuss is my future nephew that you're carrying. This is going to mean some big changes for you," Alana reminded her sister. "Are you ready for this new life?"

Adrienne smiled as she assembled the plates and silverware to lay out on the table. "This wasn't what I thought was going to happen, that's for sure. But yes, I'm ready. I have a new life inside me and since the original scenario didn't play out as planned, I've switched to plan B and I'm very cool with it."

"You're a better woman than I am, then. Because I'd be lining up lawyers from here to Timbuktu," Alana said with a frown as she expertly flipped a plump, golden omelet and slid it onto the plate that Adrienne handed her. "You agreed to be a surrogate mother to help out your friend Sierra and then she and her husband up and get divorced. Now neither one of them wants the baby and you're left holding the diaper bag. And you're okay with that?"

Adrienne shrugged as she buttered a scone. "I was remarkably naive and way too eager to play fairy godmother, no pun intended. But the baby didn't ask for any of this and I owe it to him to be a good, stable mother. And to be totally honest I was kinda getting baby fever anyway," she admitted. "I was making goo-goo eyes at every baby I saw and dreaming about being pregnant night after night. My biological clock was going tick-tick-tick and despite the circumstances, I'm quite happy about becoming a mom. It was obviously meant to be," she said calmly.

Alana raised her eyebrows and stared at Adrienne. She was sitting across the table in the sunny kitchen looking as though she didn't have a care in the world while she was carrying a baby that wasn't hers. Adrienne had always been the laid-back sister with the most open-minded outlook on life, but to be so accepting and cheerful in the midst of all this potential drama bordered on the unbelievable. Adrienne read her thoughts as usual and gave her a cheeky grin.

"Don't try to understand me, just love me. I'm very happy. I have a ton of money saved from the last two movies I did and I have full medical insurance. When my stuff gets here from LA, I'm going to move into Alexis's house and gestate until my little boy is born. I've got this, Sissie. Don't worry about me."

Alana sipped her second giant mug of coffee as she studied her sister's pretty face, which was completely serene. She was so absorbed in her examination that she almost missed Adrienne's next words.

"So that's enough deflection for the morning. Let's get back to you," she said, pointing at Alana with a piece of scone. "You can't make your annual yuletide trip to see me in Cali since I'm right here underfoot. You also can't hide out in New York with Aunt BeBe, because she's here, too. I think it's a sign that you need to do something completely different this year. This is the year that you cleanse all the angst and regret from your soul and begin to live again. I suggest you start with that hot hunk Roland Casey. He really likes you, Sissie. I had a dream about you two last night and it revealed to me that he's your soul mate," she confided.

A giant spew of coffee across the table was Alana's response, followed by coughing and sputtering as she wiped her mouth with her cloth napkin and then began wiping up the spray of coffee.

"Overreacting much?" Adrienne smiled drolly. "You know my dreams always come true, so I suggest you get ready for some happy holidays, Sis."

Alana's reply was both profane and short, which only made Adrienne laugh. "If you're not going to eat that, can I have the rest of

36

it? Your nephew is hungry."

Shoving her plate towards her greedy sister, Alana finished wiping the table and got up for more coffee.

It would have been easy to ignore Adrienne, but she was right about one thing. Her dreams were often uncannily accurate and the fact that they had both dreamed about Roland could mean something that she wasn't ready to handle, not for Christmas, New Year's or any other holiday.

Across town, Roland awoke in great spirits. He'd also had some stimulating dreams about Alana, but unlike her, he enjoyed every minute.

He stretched lazily in the bed and thought about the previous evening's activities with a smile on his face. After months of lusting in his heart for Alana Sharp Dumond he'd made real progress with her at the reception. For once she'd been open and receptive to him all night instead of being friendly but evasive.

He'd first laid eyes on her at an early-morning surprise birthday party for Alexis and she'd been sidestepping him ever since. She was always friendly and pleasant when they were in a group, but whenever he asked her out, she had other plans.

He'd been on the verge of crossing her off his to-do list permanently until she'd finally let her guard down. Once he got to hold her the way a man is supposed to hold a woman, she'd melted into his arms and he knew that Alana wasn't indifferent to him. From her immediate reaction to his touch and especially his kiss, she was as interested in him as he was in her.

Throwing back the covers, he rose from the big bed in the loft apartment he'd inherited from Jared after Jared and Alexis had moved into their spacious new house. Roland had liked the loft and the building that housed it so much that he'd bought the whole thing after he'd moved to Columbia. Real estate was a side venture of his and he never missed an opportunity for a lucrative deal. Since there was obviously going to be steady movement between Chicago and Columbia while he and the VanBurens expanded their restaurant empire, it made sense to own some living space in the city.

After his customary long stretches to limber up, Roland went to the bathroom to shower and shave, blithely ignoring his cell phone as he did so. He knew it was one or another of his sisters calling to bug him about when they would leave for Chicago and he needed a long shower and a large cup of coffee before dealing with them. He was driving the family home that day so they could celebrate the holidays with his grandparents, who hadn't made the trip down with them.

Turning on the water full blast, he stepped into the shower and cleared everything from his thoughts except Alana as he scrubbed his body under the hot spray.

She had everything he wanted in a woman; she was smart, she had a great personality and a good sense of humor. And as a bonus she was gorgeous. He'd be lying to himself if he didn't admit that he liked the way she looked, her beauty was a part of her as much as her intellect and ambition. There was something about Alana that drew him in like the song of a siren and he couldn't wait to explore that part of her more intimately.

Roland was spoiled by the women in his life, there was no doubting it. He was used to the ladies lining up to get with him, as egotistical as that may have seemed. He'd always been a good-looking guy as well as being a star athlete until a knee injury derailed his college career. But unlike many athletes, Roland didn't fall into depression and despair because he had always had a back-up plan to insure a steady income.

Besides the restaurant business, which was extremely profitable, Roland had a solid investment portfolio. His stepfather was CEO of an investment firm and he'd taught Roland and his siblings the importance of financial stability and Roland had shown a real gift for funds management. He was a triple-threat as far as women were concerned; handsome, sexy and rich and he never lacked for female companionship.

Lately, though, he'd been looking for something more substantial in his life. It had crept up on him gradually, this feeling that there was something more to life than wining, dining and bedding the beauty of the week. The feeling got more intense every time he was around Alana and he wanted to explore it to its fullest.

He turned off the shower and was about to leave the glassed-in stall when he heard a familiar voice calling to him from the living room.

"Don't come out here naked, you've got company."

He jumped and then groaned loudly. It was his nosy sister Pamela. He'd made a mistake in giving his parents the keys to his loft since she'd obviously appropriated them.

"What have I told you about coming over

when you're not invited," he yelled at her. "You're gonna get mistaken for a prowler and shot in the head if you don't watch yourself."

A chorus of giggles was all he heard as he went into the bedroom and dressed quickly in what he considered his driving clothes, a comfortable navy jogging suit that fitted his muscular body perfectly. The outfit looked fashionable and expensive. He carried his cashmere socks and his Italian driving moccasins into the living room and glared at Pam, who was in the kitchen brewing a pot of coffee.

"Why are you here?" he asked irritably.

"I came over to call shotgun," she said cheerfully. "Unlike everyone else, I packed last night and I'm ready to roll. You know how impatient I am. I can't stand being in the middle of a lot of last-minute scampering around. So I left. Where are your cups?"

He grudgingly showed her the cupboard where they were stored and sat on a bar stool to don his footwear. Despite her proclivity for making mischief, Pamela was a very organized person who was always focused on her tasks, which explained why she was ready to go while the rest of the family was still making preparations to leave the hotel.

Pam put coffee in front of him along with a plate containing a warm bagel with cream cheese and lox that she'd picked up on the way to the loft and he had to forgive her intrusion, especially when she offered to pack his bags for him. She traveled extensively in her job and she was the family pro when it came to putting a suitcase together. That didn't mean she would do it quietly, however.

"So why didn't you ask Alana to come with us to Chicago?" she asked. "I know you're gonna miss her while you're gone."

"Pamela, is there any chance that you could mind your own business for a change?"

She looked thoughtful for a moment and shook her head. "No, I don't think so. It's too out of character for me. I like knowing what's going on in everyone's lives. That's why I'm a reporter, duh."

Zipping his garment bag closed, she dusted her hands together and announced that she was finished. "We can stop by Alana's to say good-bye before we go to the hotel," she said with a dimpled grin. "Then you can lay another hot kiss on her before you disappear. That way she'll be longing for you to come back and you can pick up where you left off."

For one wild hot second, Roland thought about doing just that, but reason took over. There was no way in hell he was going to try to cop a few greedy kisses with his notoriously big-mouthed baby sister at his elbow with her handy smartphone. He would have been more than happy to grab Alana and kiss her senseless because she had the most tantalizing lips he'd ever tasted, but he wanted privacy. The concept of privacy was totally foreign to Pam.

"Just try minding your own business for five minutes, won't you please? It can be my Christmas present," he said as he picked up his bags and urged her to the door.

"Seriously? You mean I could've saved all the money I spent on you? Maybe I can return it," she said. "No, on second thought, I like getting in your business. I still say you should run by Alana's before we leave and give her something to remember you by. It's like bookmarking your favorite site on the internet."

Roland swung his overnight bag so that it hit her square in the tush. When she squeaked in outrage he mumbled, "I'd like to bookmark you. Only I'd fold you in half and stick you in a dictionary right between *pest* and *pestilence.* Let's go, woman, we've got a long drive ahead of us."

CHAPTER 3

The holidays were finally over and Alana couldn't have been more relieved. Actually, it wasn't as bad as she'd anticipated, but she was glad to see the last of the decorations disappear until next year. She stayed busy the whole time and all the activity proved to be her salvation. Between the last-minute shopping and the cooking and cleaning, she really didn't have too many spare moments to dwell on her own pain. She had to help clean Alexis's old house from top to bottom in preparation for Adrienne moving in, but that was no big deal since Alexis kept a spotless home. Her family had their big meal and gift exchange on Christmas Eve, because they were all going to cook and serve dinner at Jared's restaurant on Christmas day. It was a tradition he'd started in Chicago; all of his restaurants were open to anyone who wanted to come in for a festive meal at no charge. It was nice to have something positive to do that would take a lot of energy and focus, so she welcomed the opportunity to help.

There was a lot to keep her mind occupied between Christmas and New Year's Day, and she was grateful. There were casual gatherings at her mother's house, as well as an open house at Alexis and Jared's. She got to spend time with David Stratton, who'd been a really close friend before they'd gone off to college in two different states.

She even had two more houseguests to entertain, Sugar and Sweetie, the two Westies that belonged to Sherri Stratton's little girl. When Sherri and Lucas went on their honeymoon, his parents took Sydney to Disneyworld and Alana gladly babysat the little dogs.

Alexis had two Welsh corgis of her own, plus she and Jared took care of the elder VanBurens' corgis while they were on their trip.

It was a nice change for Alana to have the little terriers around the house because she loved dogs and she couldn't have one while she'd been married due to Sam's allergies. When she remembered this holiday she'd remember a lot of laughter, barking and eating, as well as a lot of fun.

But she was truly glad to see the last of the old year and more than ready to charge into the new year. The only thing that was bugging her right now was the dreams she kept having, night after night.

Alana didn't sleep well; she hadn't for years. She'd toss and turn for hours before drifting into a fitful sleep and when she did drop off, she would have nocturnal visits from Sam. She'd had dreams about him ever since she'd lost him and she usually woke up in tears of frustration, especially when it was one of those dreams from their past where everything was the way it used to be.

But now the dreams were taking off into another dimension altogether. She'd wake up in tears and if she could slip back into slumber she'd be treated to what seemed like hours of intensely erotic dreams, all featuring Roland. The wicked scenes of steamy sex with him were bad enough, but in addition to the sex, there were moments of tender romance so vivid that she would wake up moaning his name.

It was a mess, that's what it was. During the day she was cool, collected and in control, but her nights were leaving her disoriented, disheveled and totally distraught. Or as close to distraught as she cared to come to in this lifetime. It would have made sense for her to confide in someone, but Alana didn't even consider it. It was too embarrassing, too raw and too strange for her to verbalize. She didn't notice that the strain was beginning to show in her face, but others did.

It was a sunny morning and she was sitting at her desk in the office behind the showroom of Custom Classics, going over the week's schedule. A tap on the door preceded the entrance of Tolerance Taylor, her part-time IT specialist and full-time friend. Tolerance was known as Tollie to everyone and she was always in a great mood, smiling and talkative.

"Okay, which do you prefer, Hershey's or Dove chocolate?" Tollie asked.

"Dove," Alana answered, never taking her eyes from the computer screen.

"Star Wars or Star Trek?"

"Star Wars."

Tollie raised an arched eyebrow. "Even the set of prequels with that horrible Jar-Jar creature?"

"Yep."

"Ew. There's no accounting for taste, is there? Early-morning sex or late-night romance?" Tollie probed.

That last one made Alana turn to look at Tollie with a frown. "Where do you get these crazy questions from?"

Tollie smiled and as usual it lit up her pretty face. She was tall, plump and curvy with a stunning complexion and thick black hair that was always perfectly styled. "I told you, I get them from Facebook. Answer the question," she urged.

Alana wasn't about to go there, but she was curious. "There's a Q-and-A page on Facebook? I've never seen it."

Tollie took a seat across from Alana's desk and waved her iPad at her. "It's from that group I belong to called Building Relationships Around Reading. An amazing woman named Sharon Blount started it and it's for women who love to read and share their thoughts about books, life, love, everything. Every day there's something new and interesting, like these questions. I love them," she murmured as she continued to scan the screen. "You can really get to know people just by how they answer simple questions."

Alana turned to face Tollie with a noncommittal expression. "I doubt that. It seems like it would take a lot more than that to develop a real understanding of another person."

"Maybe. And maybe it's just as simple as

48

it seems. I'm going to ask the group about it on Saturday when we have an open chat. It's both educational and cathartic."

Alana was about to disagree when Tollie looked at her with a sheepish expression. "I came in here to let you know that there's someone here to see you and then I got caught up. Sorry about that."

"Customer or salesperson?" Without realizing it, Alana had slipped into Tollie's mode of questioning.

"Customer, definitely, but he could sell me anything. I'd buy old shoes and day-old sandwiches from him, honey," Tollie answered as her eyes locked on her screen again.

Curious, Alana went to the showroom to find Roland waiting for her with his massive arms crossed over his chest and his jaw clenched. She was surprised to see him, especially wearing an expression like that. Clearly he was upset about something and she approached with caution.

"Good morning, Roland. Can I help you with something?"

He glared down at her before answering in a snarky voice she'd never heard from him before. "Yeah, I'm here on Lucas's recommendation. I came over in person because I know from personal experience that you don't know how to answer a phone or return a message," he said. His voice was so deep that it sounded like he was growling at her.

She blushed a little because it was true; she'd been avoiding him with the skill of a spy hiding from the CIA or something. She had ignored his calls, deleted his messages and stayed away from any place she thought he might be. He'd been back in town since before the New Year and it was the first time she'd seen him and it was a week before Valentine's Day.

She looked down at his shoes because it was too hard to meet his eyes, but that was childish and she was a professional. She cleared her throat before asking him again how she could help him.

"You fix cars, right? Well, mine needs fixing," he said.

"Is it here?"

Without answering he put one of his large hands around her upper arm and led her through the showroom, taking her out the main entrance and heading to the service bay doors.

A strange sensation flooded her body as the warmth of his hand encircled the skin left bare by her short-sleeved polo shirt. It was like heat lightning ziggety-zagging all over her body, like a pinball pinging off every sensitive nerve ending she possessed. Ping, left nipple, zing, right nipple, ding-ding-ding, Miss Alana! She had to bite her lower lip to keep from giggling at the random thoughts she was having. She and her sisters always referred to their lady parts as Miss; Miss Alana, Miss Alexis and so on.

Another silly thought occurred to her and she almost choked. *Pinball or Xbox?* She'd have to spring that on Tollie one day, that is if she could still think straight after this. She was breathless when they reached the doors but she still gasped at what was waiting for her.

"Oh, Roland, I'm so, so sorry about this," she said softly.

"This" was Roland's pride and joy, his much-loved and very carefully maintained 1967 Thunderbird that had belonged to his grandfather. Roland had inherited the car from the older man and he loved it as much as, if not more than, the man who'd purchased it brand-new so many years ago. It had looked showroom-new the last time Alana had seen it; now it was all but destroyed.

The front end of the car was smashed in, along with the driver's side of the car. The glistening black finish was no more, the windshield and driver's-side window were crushed into thousands of crystal shards and the front and rear tires splayed out, a clear sign that the frame had been warped and buckled. Her heart was heavy as she surveyed the damage. She could only imagine how Roland was feeling. Without thinking about what she was doing, she put her arms around his waist and gave him an awkward hug.

"Were you driving when this happened? No one told me you were in an accident," she said as her large eyes locked with his.

His bad mood was already apparent but her soft words seemed to trip his anger trigger again. "Why would anybody tell you when it's obvious that you have no interest in me? That would be a waste of time, wouldn't it?"

Wow, he was really furious. Alana didn't react to his harsh words, but he showed a slight regret for his remark as he answered her question. "No, I wasn't driving when it happened. It was stolen. It was being stored in my dad's garage in Chicago and somebody decided that they needed it," he told her in a much calmer voice. "To make a stupid story short, the little jerk was racing it and ended up in a three-way collision. He barely escaped with his life and if he'd been driving anything else he'd have ended up a bloody smear on the road. But all that notwithstanding, I want to know if you can fix it."

"Of course I can," she said at once. "I have the best crew in the south and we can get it back to its original condition in no time at all. But how did it get here? It sounds as though the accident was in Chicago."

Roland was walking around the wreckage, looking lost. He was obviously not listening to a word that Alana was saying. "The insurance company totaled it out. The investigator said it was hopeless. Are you sure you can do something with it?"

He looked so forlorn that Alana went to his side and took his hand, squeezing it to get his attention. "Roland, dear heart, I promise you that this car can and will be restored to all its former beauty. It'll take a few weeks, but I won't let you down, truly I won't."

She finally penetrated his fog and he gave her a weak smile. "You probably think I'm a big fool for acting like this, but this was my granddad's ride. I love it almost as much as I loved him. That's why I had it hauled down here, because I saw what you did to Lucas's old Range Rover. If you could make that scrap heap look brand-new I figured there might be a chance for Black Beauty."

"Black Beauty?"

His finely planed cheekbones reddened as he admitted that his car was indeed named as such.

"People who love their cars always name them," Alana assured him. "My crew will work wonders with your baby, so rid your mind of all concern. I appreciate your trust in me and Custom Classics and we will not let you down. Come inside and let me introduce you to the people who'll be restoring Beauty. Everything's going to be fine," she added in a soothing voice.

Roland had always loved the sound of Alana's voice and he trusted her skills implicitly. But right now, more than anything else, he loved the feel of her hand in his because she hadn't let go of him and he saw no reason to change that.

Roland was totally impressed with Custom Classics, and even more impressed with its owner. The place was immaculately clean, with polished windows and floors and not a speck of dust or clutter anywhere. The retail area of the showroom was neatly organized and labeled for easy shopping; the lounge area for customers was furnished with comfortable chairs, a flat-screen TV, a coffee bar and vending machines. Everything exceeded expectations for an automotive facility; there was nothing that wasn't up-to-date and state-of-the-art in the building.

Even her staff was top-of-the-line. He met the mechanics, a tall redhead named Rachel, a middle-aged man named Lorenzo and a young woman who looked like a runway model without the makeup and ridiculous heels. Her name was Tasha and she was as business-minded as she was gorgeous.

He was also properly introduced to Tollie, who gave him an open, inquisitive smile that showed curiosity but no flirtation, which was a refreshing change of pace for him.

By the time he'd met all the men and women who worked in the different areas, from body work to interiors to specialty painting, he was sure that if anyone could reassemble his dream car, it was the Custom Classics team of experts. He said as much to Alana as they walked back to her office.

"I'm actually feeling much better now. I've been in an incredible funk since it happened. It was just out of the blue, completely unexpected. I know it sounds ridiculous, but when I got the call about Black Beauty it was like hearing that someone had died. It was a tragedy, even though that's a really extreme word for a car wreck. I thanked God that nobody was killed or seriously injured, but it was still like the worst thing that ever happened to me. I'm embarrassed to be telling you all this stuff, but the truth is the light," he said quietly.

Alana invited him to sit down on the sofa and she sat next to him, putting her hand over his. Her next words surprised him.

"You really loved your grandfather, didn't you? And that car was a part of him, a symbol of everything he meant to you. Tell me about him."

Roland's eyes lit up as he began regaling Alana with stories about the man who was such a huge part of his life. Talking to her was an incredibly cathartic experience, primarily because she was an active and attentive listener. But it was also because this was what he'd wanted, a chance to really be with her, get to know her. It would have been better if he hadn't been rambling on like a loser dude in a chick flick, emoting all over the place about a damned car, of all things. It was time to regroup and quick.

"Thanks for listening to me, Alana, I appreciate it. And I really appreciate you and your crew handling my car. Let me take you to dinner," he said. "It's the least I can do."

Alana didn't hesitate in giving him an answer, although it wasn't the one he wanted to hear. "I'd love to, Roland, but this is take-out night. Adrienne is still staying with me and I don't know if you've had much experience with pregnant women, but her mouth is set for barbecue and it wouldn't be safe for me to thwart her hormonal taste buds."

"Some other time, then," he said with a decidedly cool tone of voice. Okay, so she was shutting him down again. He rose and was about to leave when she surprised him again.

"If you don't mind hanging out with me and Adrienne, how about coming over to my place for dinner? You can take me out for an expensive meal some other time," she added teasingly.

Pow, just like that, there she was — the funny, outgoing woman he hadn't seen since the wedding. She walked him to the door and she gave him directions to her house.

Roland left Custom Classics feeling much better than when he'd arrived. Black Beauty was in good hands and he was finally making a move in the right direction with Alana. Things were looking up.

A few hours later, Adrienne was finishing

setting three places on the dining room table when the doorbell rang. She smiled and went to answer it. It had to be Roland, since she'd sent Alana out on an errand. It was Roland, looking good and smelling very nice. He was bearing gifts, too: a bouquet of flowers and two bottles of wine, one alcohol-free just for her.

"How nice! Please come in and have a seat. Alana will be right back. Let me take those for you," she said as she held out her hands for his gifts. "You can put your jacket in the closet right there," she added.

After stowing his jacket, Roland looked around Alana's living room. It was elegant and stylish, looking like something that came out of a fancy magazine.

The colors were what really caught his attention; Alana or whoever had decorated the room had a very artistic eye. Most of the colors in the room came from the paintings that were cleverly arranged on the walls. There was a fireplace wall with a glass mantel that also displayed photographs and he went over to examine them.

He recognized them as family pictures, showing Alana's sisters and her parents over the years. He was smiling at a picture of a much younger Alana combing Ava's hair when he noticed a striking shot of Alana and a man who was obviously in love with her. They were in love with each other, judging by the glowing smiles on their faces and the unmistakable look of love in their eyes.

"That's Alana and Samson, her husband," Adrienne said softly. She'd come back into the room as quietly as a cat. Her soft voice might have startled him, had he not been studying the portrait so carefully. "She always said the day she met him was the best day of her life." She paused a moment and looked at the picture before adding, "The worst day of her life was the day he died."

Roland finally understood what people meant when they said they felt like they'd been hit by a sledgehammer. It was like all the wind had been knocked out of his body for a few seconds. He was trying to think of something to say, but words failed him. What was the proper protocol when someone gave you information like that? Luckily, Adrienne kept talking.

"He was her college sweetheart. They ran off and got married in front of a justice of the peace the day after she graduated. Mama and Daddy were so mad," she laughed. "But they were very happy together. They did everything together, even their business. Custom Classics was Sam's dream and she worked with him to make it come true. For a long time I didn't think she'd get over the pain of losing him."

Clearing his throat, Roland tried to level the conversational playing field. "Sorry to hear about her loss. I can see that she's a very strong lady," he mumbled.

"Strong, but not invincible. Everyone needs someone in their life, that special someone who loves them and cares for them, someone who holds them tight at the end of a long day. Sissie is one of the strongest women I know, but it's not everything . . ." Adrienne's voice trailed off and she raised both her hands in a gesture of helplessness.

After a moment of silence, Roland asked, "Where did she get all these paintings? She must really like art."

"She loves it. And to answer your question, Alana painted all of these. She's a very talented artist, as you can see. She majored in art. Aren't they beautiful?"

"That doesn't even begin to describe it," he mumbled as he began to examine a nearby landscape more carefully. Now that he understood that the art was Alana's creation, the decor of the room made even more sense.

Furnished mainly in mid-century modern,

she'd made it eclectic enough so that it didn't look pretentious. The long sofa was oyster-white, along with the matching chaise. There were two comfortable-looking chairs in a rich turquoise color, and colorful throw pillows made the colors in the room seem to surround the space with life and light.

The walls were a soft taupe with a gray base and it served as a perfect backdrop for the brilliant colors of the pictures. The dark hardwood floors gleamed and wicker baskets topped with glass served as end tables. The wicker and the big green plants positioned around the room made it even more vibrant.

Roland couldn't remember being in a room that he liked as well as this one, and he normally paid very little attention to things like decorating. This place was special, though, as special as the woman who put it all together.

Alana came in through the kitchen just then, calling out to Adrienne. "I got your prenatal vitamins, but the pharmacist said you can't get the prescription filled yet because it's too early. He was really snippy about it, too," she said. She'd reached the living room by then, still talking while trying to take her coat off with one hand as she shifted her shoulder bag and the pharmacy bag in the other. She stopped walking and her eyes widened once she realized that Roland was standing in her living room.

"Oh, you're here," she said, looking adorably flustered.

He moved to her side where he quickly helped with the coat and gallantly held her bag. "I just got here. Adrienne was showing me your artwork. You are some kind of artist, Alana. I've never seen anything like these outside of a gallery or a museum," he told her as he returned the bag to her and went to the closet to hang up her coat.

"Thank you, Roland. That's very nice of you. Sorry I was late, but my nephew needs his nourishment, or whatever you call vitamins." She tossed the pharmacy bag to Adrienne who squeaked as she made a fumbling catch.

"You still catch like a girl," Alana teased her.

"And you still throw like a man, Sissie. You don't know your own strength."

Roland grinned. "This sounds like being at home with my sisters. Why do you call her Sissie?"

Adrienne threw her arms around Alana and gave her a big hug. "Because she's my big sister and I couldn't manage *Alana* or *sister* when I was a baby. So she's my Sissie."

"Roland, if you ever call me that I will draw flowers all over your head with a permanent marker. This is your only warning. You guys hungry? I'm starving so let's sit down," she said as she headed for the kitchen to begin serving.

After Adrienne showed him where he could wash his hands, he joined the two ladies in the dining room. Alana thanked him sweetly for the flowers before they said grace. "Tulips are my very favorite ones," she said. "I love the way they smell."

"I didn't think they had a smell," Roland said with a quirk of his brow.

"Take a whiff and see."

He took her advice and inhaled the scent of the flowers, which Adrienne had arranged in a vase. A light, fresh fragrance caressed his nose. "Very nice." He looked at Alana, looking just as fresh and beautiful as the flowers smelled. "Very, very nice."

CHAPTER 4

"Thanks again for dinner, Alana."

After a very good meal of takeout from Sweet Tea & 3 Sides, the best rib joint in the city, Adrienne had given in to her now-typical need for a nap after most meals and gone to bed. Roland, gentleman that he was, helped Alana clean up the kitchen and put everything in order, although she told him it wasn't necessary.

"Are you like those VanBuren men who won't let a lady lift a finger? Because it's not a deal-breaker, I assure you. Although I am impressed with your skills," Alana told him.

They were relaxing in the living room with a fire going and the sound of Alabama Shakes playing. Roland took a sip of wine before answering her.

"It's kinda complicated," he said slowly. "I'm the oldest of seven, you know, and after my father — my mother's first husband

64

— disappeared, I was in charge of a horde of screaming little girls. My mother had to work two jobs, and sometimes three, to keep a roof over our heads, so I had to keep order in the house when she wasn't at home. I was the protective big brother and treated them like little ladies, which is how my mother wanted it, of course. And how I wanted it because they were my little sisters and I would have moved heaven and earth to keep them safe. I didn't want anyone looking at them cross-eyed, you know? Chicago is a rough place no matter what part of town you're in and after my father abandoned us, we had to move to a fairly undesirable area, so my role changed fast.

"I had to help them get ready for school, give them breakfast, walk them to school, pick them up afterwards and keep them from killing each other when we got home. Make sure they did their homework, fix dinner and I had to keep the house clean. My mother had enough on her plate so I had to pitch in," he said with a shrug.

Alana was awed by his story. "Wow, that's a lot of responsibility for you at a really young age. Your mother must be so proud of you. I'm proud of you and I didn't even know you back then," she said with sincerity warming her voice. She drank a little more wine as she leaned into the big pillows behind her. She rubbed the rim of her wineglass across her bottom lip in an unconsciously sexy move. "May I ask what happened to your father? I realize it's really personal and I have no right to ask, so if you don't want to talk about it, that is fine," she murmured.

Roland made a gesture to indicate that it was of no importance. "You can ask my anything you want, Alana. I have nothing to hide from you. My birth father wasn't a bad guy, I guess, just irresponsible, not ready to have so many children, immature, whatever label you want to put on him. He didn't come home from work one day and that was it. We had a nice house in the 'burbs, my mother was a teacher and he was an executive with a real estate company. We found out later that he'd been having an affair with a woman he worked with and they ran off together. He'd cleaned out the bank accounts and they headed to the west coast. They'd had a kid together, too, if you can believe that," he said, shaking his head with obvious scorn.

"That must have been extremely hard on your mother. Of course it was hard for all of you, but your mother must have been crushed."

"She was, but she couldn't afford to give in to it. That's what she used to tell me," he said. "At first I used to hear her crying every night after we went to bed and I wanted to hunt him down and kill him with my bare hands. She had to keep it together for us, of course, and she just buckled down and worked tirelessly so that we would have everything we needed. I wanted to get a job, but it was more important that I be there for the girls.

"In order to keep them focused I had to assign chores to each one of them and make them realize that we all had a role to play in the family. That's why I told you it's complicated; it would have been nice to be able to be the doting big brother and wait on the girls hand and foot like the VanBuren men, but we weren't in that position, not anymore."

Alana couldn't imagine what it must have been like for the family. Her heart ached for all the pain his mother had gone through and all the confusion and anger he must have felt. "Your mother seems really happy now," she said.

Roland's face relaxed into a huge smile. "Man, is she ever. It's ironic, but that man leaving was the best thing that could have ever happened to her. If Duane Johnson hadn't taken off, she never would have met Renard Casey. She had a part-time job at night working for a cleaning company and she met Renard when she was cleaning his offices. He took one look at her and it was all over for him. He wined her, dined her, won over her wild children and the next thing you know we were back in the 'burbs in a much bigger house, she was pregnant with my baby brother and we all lived happily ever after. He adopted us, which is why my name is Casey and not Johnson," he added.

"That's a beautiful ending for a beautiful lady," Alana said with a smile. Glendora Casey was indeed a lovely woman and even though she hadn't spent a lot of time with his parents, Renard Casey had the unmistakable look of a man who was deeply in love with his family, especially his wife. "I love that story, I really do. Do you ever see your birth father?"

"He died years ago. Never saw him again after he bailed on us. But you know what?" He leaned forward to place his glass on the coffee table.

"What?"

"I'm tired of talking about me. Let's talk about you for a change," he said in a voice as sweet as the wine they had just consumed.

A normal Alana response would have been a smart remark guaranteed to put him firmly back in his place, which would have been anywhere she wasn't. Instead she giggled like a love-hungry teenager, a pretty, rippling sound that tickled Roland's ears. She curled her long legs up on the sofa and turned so that she was fully facing him. He moved a pillow that was between them and turned so that he was closer to her, his long arm draped across the back of the sofa.

"I'm not that interesting. I can't think of one interesting thing about me. I'm a mechanic, that's all."

"Liar, liar, tight, sexy jeans on fire," he said, brushing her hair away from her face. "You're not a mechanic; you're an artist and a damned good one. You're funny and sweet and incredibly beautiful. You're full of it, Alana."

Mock outrage and merriment filled her eyes and she aimed a small fist at him as if she were going to punch his chin. "That's a fine way to talk, Roland!"

He took her hand in his and kissed it. "You didn't let me finish. I was about to say that you're full of mystery, charm, sweetness and sensuality. See what happens when you don't let a man finish a sentence?"

"That's really sweet, but I think you're the one who's full of it now and I don't mean mystery." She giggled madly as he wrapped his arms around her and planted a kiss on the corner of her mouth.

"Are you coming on to me?" She tried to look stern but failed.

"Is it working? 'Cause if it is, I am."

They both laughed and she relaxed into his embrace.

"You really are a woman of mystery, though. Why aren't you painting anymore? Your work is fantastic, Alana. I've never seen anything like it."

"I do paint. I paint cars," she said pertly.

"I'm serious," he protested. "You're a real artist. Why aren't you pursuing your art?"

"I haven't quit painting, not completely. I have a studio and everything. Would you like to see it?"

"Of course I would." He kissed her cheek and she turned slightly so that their mouths met. It started out slowly, just their lips touching. His tongue outlined her lips and she returned the favor until they were kissing deeply and deliberately, sucking and stroking passionately before Roland broke it off. He tightened his arms around her and made a deep sound that was part passion and part deep regret. "Let's go see that studio right now before we do something we might regret."

Without waiting for an answer he stood up and pulled her to her feet.

"That's a great idea," Alana said breathlessly.

Her studio was in a sunroom located next to the family room. It was the perfect spot for a studio because it had floor-to-ceiling windows on three sides. It was as tidy as the parts of the house he'd already seen and it looked very organized.

"You weren't kidding about your painting," he said. There was a large stretched canvas on a tall easel that bore a portrait of Adrienne looking radiant and obviously pregnant. It wasn't finished, but it was already a stunning work of art. The one wall that didn't have windows served as a gallery of sorts; there were lots of unframed pieces in oil, watercolor and pastels. A big slanted worktable held a sketchbook with colored pencil drawings. It caught his attention and he went over to take a closer look.

"This is adorable," he said. "That's Sydney, isn't it?"

"Yes, it's a book I'm making for her. She told me about a dream she had about something called 'Oom-Fala Pie' and it was so cute that I started making her a little book." She turned the pages so he could see her progress.

"I'm not an expert on kids' books, but this is the cutest thing I've ever seen. You're amazing."

The book showed Sydney and Lucas making a fabulous pie for Sherri, with the help of Sugar and Sweetie, the little Westies. It was colorful and engaging and there was a recipe in the back, along with a little song. Roland was totally taken with the book.

"How does the song go?"

"I'll sing it for you if you promise not to laugh," she said. "Okay, here goes: Oh, my, Oom-Fala pie, if you never had it you should give it a try! It's good for girls and it's good for guys, so have yourself some Oom-Fala Pie!" Her face was flushed and she laughed as she finished the little ditty.

"You know what?"

"What?"

A loud noise followed by a yelp made them both jump. Alana's eyes widened and she left the studio, headed for the kitchen with Roland on her heels. They were greeted by the sight of Adrienne hopping on one foot with a frown on her face.

"Don't pay me any attention," she said crossly. "I had a sudden urge for water-

72

melon and I dropped it on my foot. I should have cut it up before I put it in the refrigerator."

In minutes Roland had retrieved the errant melon and sliced it up before cutting it into manageable cubes, while Alana made her sister sit down and examined her foot. She made an ice pack out of a bag of frozen peas and made her put her foot up on a small stool.

"I didn't mean to interrupt your evening, but I do appreciate the attention," Adrienne said gratefully.

"Think nothing of it," Roland said easily. "And actually I think it's time that I hit the road. It's getting late. Thanks again for your hospitality, Adrienne."

She waved goodbye with a chunk of melon and Alana walked him to the door. She took his jacket out of the closet and handed it to him.

"Thanks again, Alana. I had a great time."

"You're more than welcome, Roland. I enjoyed myself, too."

"So what's on your agenda for the rest of the week?"

"It's a busy week for me. Adrienne's furniture is getting here tomorrow and I'll be helping her get moved in. And Alexis and Jared's anniversary party is this weekend, and . . ."

Her words stopped as Roland covered her mouth with his. It was a long, sweet kiss with just the right amount of tenderness. He tipped her chin up and gazed down at her. "Then I'll see you tomorrow. I couldn't let two beautiful women handle a big moving job by themselves. And I'll definitely see you this weekend. We can go to the party together."

Without waiting for her answer he kissed her again and left without another word. She was still standing in the doorway when Adrienne came to find her. She had a bowl of watermelon in one hand and was guiding another piece to her mouth.

"This was fun, Sissie. We've got to do this again."

Alana shook herself and walked over to the sofa, sitting down hard as if all her bones had dissolved. Adrienne curled up next to her, plucking another chunk of the cold red melon in her fingertips. "What's the matter with you? You look kinda dazed or something."

Alana took the juicy bite away from her sister and popped it in her mouth. "I think I'm getting in way over my head, Adrienne. Way, way over my head. Tonight was a huge mistake."

■ ■ ■ ■

Luckily, the next few days were so busy that Alana didn't have time to dwell on her so-called mistake.

She and Adrienne had a talk while they polished off the rest of the watermelon and Adrienne had assured her that she had no reason to feel conflicted over spending a pleasant evening with a nice man. Alana had mostly listened, since Adrienne did most of the talking.

They didn't talk for very long because a big bowl of melon combined with a pregnant woman's bladder meant that a bathroom break took priority over everything else, so when nature called they went to bed. And surprisingly, Alana slept all night without her usual triple-X movie features. Her dream was rather sweet and funny for a change, all about Sydney's dogs dancing around with little hats on while Sydney sang the Oom-Fala song. There was something about a pile of books on a big table covered with a hot pink cloth and a crowd of people smiling and clapping and both Sam and Roland were there, which was just crazy, but she didn't wake up sobbing and sweaty for a change.

Moving day was relatively easy because everyone turned out to help. Roland was there, along with Jared and Alexis and a few guys from the restaurant. Tollie came to lend a hand, too, and with so many people, the unpacking and furniture arranging went rapidly.

Of course, it was due mostly to Aretha's supervision. Alana's mother, Aretha Sharp, was the reason that all the Sharp sisters were so tidy and organized. Aretha could make a plan and execute it faster than anyone and she had things moving like clockwork. She even managed to corral Ava, the youngest of the sisters, into being a valuable asset to the process. Ava kept the cold drinks coming, picked up the lunch and snacks for everyone and was responsible for breaking down the boxes as they were emptied.

Alexis was on kitchen duty, putting all the dishes and utensils in the dishwasher before putting them away. Due to her pregnancy, it was all Jared would let her do and he wasn't thrilled about even that light activity. He kept coming to check on her, making sure she was comfortable and not overdoing it.

Alana watched the two of them in action with a thoughtful look on her face. When he departed to help assemble Adrienne's bed, she had a question for her sister.

"Do you ever feel like Jared babies you too much?" Alana asked curiously.

"Nope, not a bit. He's perfect for me," Alexis assured her. "I like being pampered and he likes to pamper me so it's a win-win. Besides, I give as good as I get," she said with a very private smile.

"Oh. I was just wondering," Alana said lamely.

"Wondering about what? About abandoning your independence to a strong man in a committed relationship? Because it's not that cut-and-dried, I can tell you that," Alexis said. "You know what I mean. Look at you and Sam. I remember how you were with him and how he was with you. Don't worry, Alana. I know it's been a long time for you but you'll be just fine."

Alana's confusion showed on her face. "What are you talking about?"

"I'm just saying that you had a deep, loving relationship with a man who adored you, who took care of you and understood you, and the best part is that he allowed you to return those feelings. You've been on your own for a long time and you're used to that, but when the right man comes into your life you'll be able to have that again," she said.

"Alana, how about we take a break for a while? You've been working for hours and you could use a time out." Roland had entered the kitchen with the silent grace of a panther and as he spoke, he took a stack of large baking utensils out of Alana's arms and put them on the designated shelf.

Alexis beamed happily as Roland took Alana's hand to lead her off for a brief respite from the hubbub of boxes, crates, bubble wrap and the like.

Alana, on the other hand, looked like a woodland creature staring down the high beams of a fast-moving semitruck. Her cell phone rang and she snatched it out of her pocket and answered it as fast as humanly possible.

"Hello?" she said breathlessly. "Oh, yeah, no problem, Mama, I'll do it right now."

She raised her hands helplessly and mumbled something about running an errand for Aretha. Before Roland could stop her, she was gone. He looked to Alexis for an explanation.

"Did I do something wrong?"

Alexis shook her head. "No, dear, you're doing something right. It's time for us to have a little talk, Roland. In fact, it's a little overdue. Why don't you come over for dinner tonight and I'll remedy that."

Roland thought about it for a minute or two before saying no-thanks. "I appreciate it, Alexis, but I think this is something that Alana and I are going to have to work through on our own. I don't know her as well as I intend to, but I don't think she'd like the idea of me getting information about her secondhand. She's not ready to confide in me yet, and I can handle that. For right now, I'll just keep doing what I'm doing until she tells me to stop."

Alexis smiled tearfully. "If I wasn't so pregnant I'd get off this stool and give you a big hug, Roland. You know what you're doing."

"I could have met you there, Roland. There was no reason for you to come all the way over here to get me," Alana said as she greeted him at the door.

"There was every reason," Roland contradicted her. "I always pick up my date, for one thing. For another thing, I wanted to see your smile when I gave you these," he said as he handed her a stunning arrangement of tulips in a thick crystal vase.

They were a beautiful shade of orange and

they were so perfect they almost didn't look real. Alana's smile did, however; it was easy to see that she was touched and very pleased with them. "Roland, these are absolutely beautiful. Thank you so much," she said.

"There it is! That's the look I wanted to see. I love that smile of yours. And the other reason I wanted to come over to get you was because I wanted to be the first one to see how gorgeous you look."

Alana thanked him with a bashful smile. She was casually attired in slim-fitting jeans and an ivory cashmere sweater with a big cowl neck. Her only jewelry was an armful of silver bangle bracelets and big silver hoop earrings. Soft black ballet flats completed her simple but sexy outfit.

"You're looking pretty handsome yourself. Let me put these on the coffee table and get my coat and we can go."

The anniversary party was festive and homey at the same time. They were greeted at the door by Alexis's dogs, who considered themselves the hostesses of every gathering. Alexis and Jared were both aglow with happiness, the same way they'd been at their wedding. Her parents were there, and Jared's were, too, all full of joy over marking the couple's first year of marriage.

Alana was happy, too; how could she not

be, seeing the way Jared looked at her sister with so much love and tenderness? Incipient motherhood was extremely becoming to Alexis, she thought. She'd always been a pretty woman, but with the love and caring that she and her husband lavished on each other, Alexis looked absolutely beautiful. Jared obviously thought so, too, because he was always near her, touching her in some way. It was particularly sweet when he would place his hand on their baby-to-be and then say something meant for her alone. The way her face would light up would have been a little saccharine on anyone else, but on Alexis it looked just perfect.

Lucas and Sherri were equally blissful. The brand-newlyweds also couldn't stay away from each other. Sherri's brother David couldn't make it from D.C., but her parents were there, which was different, but nice. Ever since Sherri's ex-fiancé, Trevor Barnes, who was Sydney's biological father, had shown up in Columbia and tried to weasel his way back into Sherri's life, things had changed radically between Sherri and her cold, conservative parents. Once they realized that Trevor was, as Lucas put it, "bat-shit crazy", the walls that had always been between the Strattons and their children had come tumbling down.

The Strattons were much warmer and more human now; they doted on their granddaughter Sydney so much that Sherri feared she'd get spoiled, but so far she was still a little angel. The change in her parents was amazing. Mrs. Stratton was not only smiling and being friendly to everyone, she'd had her hair cut into a becoming style and she was wearing a pretty pink sweater with a matching pair of slacks. Her old wardrobe had been all beige, all the time.

Alana was quietly observing everyone from her seat in a double-sized armchair next to Roland. It was a great party. Everyone was relaxed and having fun. The love that was flowing around the room was almost visible to the naked eye. People were starting to make toasts, which were funny and touching at the same time.

When it was Jared's turn, he stood behind his wife with his arms around her, kissing her on the cheek before he began. His blond hair was artfully styled, thanks to Alexis, and his blue-green eyes sparkled with joy as he began speaking.

"We want to thank everyone for coming over to celebrate our first year of marriage. For me, it's been the most amazing time of my life. My wife is the best gift I've ever gotten and the beautiful baby inside her makes me love her even more. I've been very blessed, and I know it. I have a great family, great friends and a career that I thoroughly enjoy," he said.

Sookie and Honeybee barked indignantly and everyone laughed. "And we have two of the most amazing dogs in the world who never let me forget it," he said with a laugh. "But I can tell you that nothing in my entire life has ever meant as much to me as the love and trust and respect of the beautiful lady with whom I will spend the rest of my life."

He turned her around to face him, cupping her face with one hand. "I love you more every day and I thank you every day for loving me. Happy Anniversary, beauty."

Everyone was applauding and tears were flowing and it was just a really sweet thing to witness. Alana was as touched as everyone else, although she couldn't ignore a hot pang in her heart. She was happy for her sister's happiness and no one deserved it more than she did, unless it was Sherri. And as though the universe was agreeing with her, another toast came a few minutes later. Lucas stood in the center of the room with Sydney on his hip and his arm around Sherri. He was looking proud and happy, like the king of the world when he began speaking.

"We want to congratulate Jared and Alexis and wish them a lifetime of continued happiness. And we want to share some happiness with everyone. When Sherri and I went on our honeymoon, which was incredible, by the way, we brought back a lot of gifts and souvenirs for our little girl. But we also brought her the one she really wanted and she wants to tell you what it is, don't you, cutie?"

Sydney nodded emphatically and said, "Yes, I do. My mommy and daddy brought me a baby brother! He won't be here for a while, but he's coming. Isn't that great?"

More laughter, applause and tears of joy erupted around the room, accompanied by happy barking. It was a true celebration in every sense of the word for everyone but Alana. The pang in her heart was turning into an unbearable pain and she prayed that no one noticed that her tears weren't from happiness, but from a long-denied sense of loss and loneliness.

There was so much happy chatter and laughter that no one paid her any attention, no one but Roland.

CHAPTER 5

"What a great night," Alana said cheerfully. "It was a wonderful party. I couldn't tell who was the happiest about the baby news, the VanBurens or the Strattons. Sydney was adorable, wasn't she?"

Roland had been listening to Alana chatter ever since they'd left the party and he let her go on, even though it wasn't like her at all. The ride home didn't take long, but she talked the whole time. He turned into her driveway and after helping her out of the car, he walked her to the door. Her eyes had an unnatural sheen to them and it was evident that she was holding on to her composure by a thread.

"Umm, well, good night, Roland. Thanks for coming with me and umm . . ."

"Aren't you going to ask me in for coffee or a glass of wine or something?"

Alana blinked. "Sure, why not? Come on in," she mumbled.

"Why don't you turn on the fire and put on some music and I'll make you a fantastic drink. Do you have any brandy?"

"I'm pretty sure I do. It's in the cabinet next to the refrigerator."

"You relax and I'll be right back."

When he returned with two pottery mugs of a delicious-smelling drink, Alana was curled up in a corner of the sofa looking melancholy but resolute. The fire was flickering and an old Al Jarreau CD was playing. He handed a mug to her and she took it, murmuring her thanks. He sat down and watched her take her first sip of his version of Irish coffee.

"This is really good, Roland. Thanks again."

"You're more than welcome, Alana. Anything you want, anytime you want it, honey."

They sat in silence for a few minutes until Roland could sense that she'd relaxed a bit. He put his mug on the coffee table and moved closer to her, putting his arm around her shoulders. She gave him a weak imitation of her usual smile and handed her mug to him.

"I think I've had enough for right now."

"That's fine. I'll make you some more later if you'd like. I'll do anything for you, Alana."

She moved so that her head was on his shoulder and she rubbed her face on his broad shoulder. "Really? Anything?"

"As long as you do one thing for me. Tell me what made you so sad tonight, honey. I know you were happy for your sister and for Sherri, but I could feel your heart breaking. Talk to me, Alana."

He felt her slender body go absolutely still and her sharp intake of breath before he placed her in his lap and held her as close as he could. "It's okay, Alana, you can tell me, honey."

He wasn't really prepared for the sob that issued from deep inside her, but it didn't put him off in any way. All he wanted to do was comfort her, to make her realize that he was there for her and always would be. He'd hold her forever if that's what it took for her to lower her guard and let him in. It was as though a curtain had been lifted in a dark room and revealed everything that had been hidden from his view up until now.

What he saw was his heart and his future; he was holding the rest of his life in his arms.

Her broken cries slowed down and gradually stopped. Oddly, the next sound he heard was a loud sniffle and a cracked little laugh.

"I need you to close your eyes while I go

wash my face," she mumbled. "Otherwise there's a real good chance that I'm going to leave a nasty trail of mascara and lip gloss all over your beautiful sweater."

It was such an unexpected remark that Roland couldn't stop the deep belly laugh that came out. He tried to kiss her and ended up kissing her hands because she'd covered her face. "C'mon, honey girl, just one kiss to seal the deal. You can't look bad to me; just let me give you one little kiss."

While he was pleading his case Alana wriggled away from him and ran to the bathroom. She was back in minutes with a squeaky-clean face and a box of tissues. She returned to her place in his lap armed with a handful of tissues and a small sigh.

"I'm sorry about that. I never, ever do that," she confessed.

"You don't have to apologize to me for anything," Roland said firmly. His long fingers stroked the side of her face as he reassured her. "I know something affected you deeply tonight and I want to make you feel better. I don't know you well enough to try to guess, but I want to. I want to know you so well that you feel like you can tell me anything, anytime, anywhere. I want you to realize that I'm always going to be here for you, always."

Alana didn't say anything for a moment. She was looking into his eyes, staring so intensely that he was sure that she could see his soul looking back at her. When she started to speak, it was in a slow, measured voice as though she wanted to make sure that he comprehended every word. Her hand rested on his chest, smoothing the fine purple merino knit over and over.

"This life, the one I have now, isn't the one I planned on," she began. "I met Samson Dumond my junior year of college and he was it for me. We came together like magnets and we just never let go. We completed each other, we made each other whole or whatever they say in romance novels.

"From the very beginning we knew we'd be together forever and our future was all planned," she said, her eyes misting over with the memories. "Our parents weren't happy that we eloped, especially my mother. She flipped out when we came back here married, but she got over it. Eventually," she added with a wry smile.

"He'd majored in automotive engineering, but the market was so bad when he graduated that he came up with the idea for Custom Classics. I was working with him until the business got on its feet, and then I was going to grad school so that I could teach art while I built up my sales and my client base as a portrait artist. We had it all planned and it was working, too. Custom Classics caught on like wildfire and things were going just the way we wanted." She stopped to blot her eyes and swallowed hard before continuing.

"Right before Christmas, we decided to get a big live tree. We'd closed up the shop and went to the bank to make a deposit. We always deposited the bags at night so there wouldn't be any money in the store overnight. We were both driving that day because I'd had a doctor's appointment, so Sam followed me to the bank when I made the drop. He was watching my back, like he always did. He was behind me, but a car got between us, because I didn't see him when I got there. I was about to get out of the car when a man grabbed my arm and jerked me out of the driver's seat.

"I can't say for sure what happened next. Everything went so fast. All I know for sure is that Sam came up out of nowhere and went for the man, who had a gun. And the gun went off and Sam was shot. I must have jumped in at some point because I got shot, too.

"When I came to I was in the hospital.

My husband was gone and so was our baby. And that was the end of my life. You can plan for everything, for a marriage, a career, a house, children, you can plan it all out, but one random meth-head can destroy everything just like that," she said, snapping her fingers. "Just like that."

Roland was stunned and humbled by what he was hearing. Now he knew why Alana was so elusive, why she ran hot and cold with no warning. She hadn't gotten over the pain and the anguish she'd suffered from losing her husband and their baby. And that was why she reacted the way she had at the party. It must be killing her to see her sisters and her friends living the life she should have had with her first love. And to have to stand on the sidelines and watch while they celebrated the babies they were having.

He could imagine her pain; he knew the kind of strength it took to rebuild and keep living when your world had crumbled around your feet. He'd seen what it had done to his mother. His hand stroked her silky hair and he tried to think of the most eloquent thing to say.

"Alana, I . . ."

"I'm sure that's more than you ever wanted to know about me," she said ruefully, patting her eyes with the wadded-up tissues. "I just couldn't stop once I started talking. I never talk about it, you know. It's too depressing for other people to hear. They start making these pained faces and their eyes dart left and right like they're looking for an escape hatch. Anything to get away from the poor sad lady." She laughed mirthlessly.

"I wallowed in misery for a while and then I just stopped. My mother and my sisters, especially Adrienne, they were there for me and they kept telling me that Sam wouldn't want me to give up. That he'd want me to keep on living, to pull it together and to be happy again.

"So I did. I went back to work and I built Custom Classics up into what Sam wanted it to be. I'm sure he's proud of it; that place meant everything to him. He died trying to protect the deposit and it would've been really weak of me not to keep it going. I have a good life. I have a lot to be grateful for; I don't want you to think that I don't know that. But it's not the life I wanted; it's the life I got."

Roland wanted to contradict her; Sam died protecting her, the woman he loved, not the stupid deposit. He wanted to tell her that she was living her late husband's dreams, not hers. But he didn't want to come across preachy and paternal because she hadn't asked for his advice, just his listening ear. He'd asked her to talk to him, to confide in him and that's what she'd done. What came next had to be up to her.

"What can I do to help, Alana? I don't want you to feel like you're alone anymore," he said. He tilted her chin up so that their eyes met. "You've been handling a whole lot of things by yourself, from what I can tell, and it's time for that to be over. It's time for a new life for you."

They leaned into each other at the same time and the resulting kiss started out tender and binding, but it soon turned hot and passionate. Her hands slid up his broad shoulders and she locked her arms around his neck, while his went down her body, sliding under the soft sweater until she could feel him against her bare skin. She moved against him urgently, changing positions until she was straddling him and they were beginning to get lost in each other. Alana managed to slow down, gently pulling away from his lips.

"Stay with me, Roland. Stay with me tonight," she whispered.

CHAPTER 6

Take one step forward and six steps back.
That was exactly how Alana felt ever since
the night of the anniversary party. She'd
opened her soul to Roland because that's
what he'd said he wanted. He wanted her
to talk, and she'd talked. He wanted to get
to know her better, to know what made her
tick, to let her know she wasn't alone
anymore. But after she'd poured out the
things she'd been keeping inside her for so
long, he'd bolted.

She'd asked him to stay the night with her
and he'd run like he'd stolen something.
Her face still got hot every time she thought
about how embarrassing it was to offer
herself up to him like that only to get turned
down flat.

And she thought about it fairly often
because it was a big thing to her, monumen-
tal, as a matter of fact. She spent her days
trying to hide her anger and disappoint-

ment, and her nights staying awake. Sleep was just out of the question. It might have been her insomnia but she knew it wasn't; it was because she was afraid of what might come to her in her dreams. The only up side was the fact that she was getting a lot of painting done.

Every night she'd go into the studio and paint until the sun came up and it was time to get ready to go to work. Yes, she was going through the motions of living, but she'd had plenty of practice doing that. Her painting had become her lifeline because it was the only way she could stop thinking about the night that Roland had left her flat.

During the day, the horrible scene was always right there, right under the surface of whatever she was doing. When she was at Custom Classics she was pleasant and professional as always and no one could sense that anything was amiss, that is except for Tolerance.

Tollie was even more intuitive than Adrienne and she could sense a big change in her friend. Alana knew that Tollie was trying to find out what was on her mind and she also knew it would only be a matter of time before she pried it out of her. Sometimes she was convinced that Tollie was a witch.

Sure enough, Tollie came into her office with a determined look on her face. "I'm taking you to lunch and we're going to talk because there's something on your mind and it's making you crazy. C'mon, let's go."

As if she had no power over her own feet, Alana got her coat and purse and within minutes they were seated in a back booth at their favorite little sandwich shop. Tollie had already called in their orders which appeared with big glasses of sweet tea. Once their waiter left the table, Tollie leaned over and said, "Talk."

When Alana hesitated, Tollie reached over and took her hand. "Alana, you look like you haven't slept in three days. You haven't been eating right, either, I can tell. A chubby chick always knows when her skinny friend has lost weight she can't spare and your clothes are starting to hang on you. Your hair has lost its sheen and you have Lipton-sized bags under your eyes. I haven't seen you look like this since Sam passed away."

It was a sign of how far gone Alana was; the fact that her expression didn't change when Tollie used Sam's name. It was like an unspoken agreement among her friends and relatives not to talk about Sam because it always seemed to make Alana feel bad. Tollie pushed her advantage by squeezing

Alana's hand.

"Alana, I can't let you slip back into the abyss. You can't let whatever is bothering you make you lose yourself again. Talk to me, girl. And do it now, people are looking at us like you're breaking up with me or something."

Alana actually managed a laugh at that remark and she took her hand back. She took a sip of her tea and a small bite of her Cobb salad, and then she began talking. She told Tollie about the party and how Roland brought her home and urged her to unburden herself. She held back none of the details, right up until the point where she'd asked him to stay and he'd left abruptly.

Tollie looked puzzled. "So you two were kissing and getting hot and bothered and then he just turned and ran after you asked him to stay?"

"Pretty much," Alana said grumpily.

"I need to know precisely what happened," Tollie pressed. "What exactly went on from the time you said 'stay with me' until the moment he put his hand on the doorknob to leave?"

Alana stabbed a piece of avocado with her fork and put it in her mouth before answering. "We kissed some more and he picked me up and carried me into the bedroom.

97

He put me on the bed and he was about to pull off his sweater and all of a sudden he stopped. He sat down on the bed and told me it was too soon for us and that I needed to be sure that this is what I wanted. And then he left." She shrugged to indicate it was of no importance but Tollie knew better.

"Alana, is that giant portrait you painted of Sam still hanging over your bed?"

"Yes, of course it is."

"And all those photos and drawings of him still all over the walls?"

"Yes, they are. Ever since I moved into the house, they've been there."

"Sweetie, no matter how much a man cares for you, no matter how much he loves you, he's not gonna be able to make love to you in a shrine and that's what your bedroom is. You can't blame him for losing the urge to merge, honey. Once he saw that elaborate tribute to your late husband, he got out of the mood when he realized that you're still in love with Sam."

Alana immediately got defensive. "I can have anything I want in my bedroom," she snapped. "And of course I still love Sam. He was my husband, my life! Am I just supposed to stop loving him because some low-down bastard killed him?"

Tollie's face softened. "Honey baby, of course you still love him. You'll always have love for him. But to still be in love with him is something else. That means there's no room for someone else in your heart or in your life and from what I've seen of Roland, he's not one to share. That man has real feelings for you, Alana. He wants you to share your life with him and that's going to mean giving up the life you had with Sam. It's time for you to start living on your own."

Alana looked stunned at her friend's words. "That's exactly what I've been doing since the minute I woke up and was told my husband was dead and I'd lost our baby," she said bitterly.

"You've been living, but it's not your life, not completely. The only reason you moved into your house was because that management company sold your apartment complex and turned it into a senior living facility. If it wasn't for that you'd still be living there with everything in place the way it was when you lived with Sam.

"Custom Classics is a very nice business and you've done very well with it, but it wasn't your chosen career. You had a totally different career mapped out for yourself and you abandoned it completely after Sam died. You can't tell me that the way you're living would make Sam happy. He'd want you to move on and be happy and fulfilled. I believe that from the bottom of my heart, I really do. I want you to be happy, too. And I also believe that Roland can make you happy. That is if you let him."

"I doubt that I'll be seeing him again, at least not on a personal basis."

"You haven't heard from him at all? I find that hard to believe."

"I haven't talked to him; I didn't say that he hadn't called me. I just haven't called him back or taken his calls. He even sent me tulips," she admitted.

"How long has it been since you had actual face time with him? The three days since the party, right? Those are the three days you haven't slept — what a co-incidence. I think you've made him suffer enough, Alana. And you've certainly suffered enough — it's all over your face. Talk to him, go out with him, and let him hug you and hold you and make you feel better like a man is supposed to. You'll be surprised at how much better you'll feel when you do," Tollie said wisely.

"Tolerance, I'm just fine," Alana protested. "There's nothing wrong with me or the way I live my life."

"If there was nothing wrong, you'd be able to sleep at night. Have you ever thought about getting counseling for your depression?"

"My what? I'm not depressed; I'm always in a good mood. Do you see me dragging around town looked run-down and ratty? No, you don't," Alana said indignantly.

"There are all kinds of ways depression can manifest itself. It's different for different people. And it's not an indictment of you or your mental state, it's a physiological thing. A chemical imbalance," Tollie said with authority. "Did you know that lots of African-American women suffer from it? And won't get counseling, either. There are two things most folks will not own up to — we ain't fat, and we ain't crazy. And because we're in denial about these things, we don't get help with them and we stress ourselves out needlessly. I'm not equating depressed to crazy, but you know what I mean.

"Now, me, I'm fat and I admit it. I'm fat because I eat too much, but I'm pretty so I get a pass. But even I've decided to take off some weight because it's getting too hard to wear my stilettos. And it doesn't make sense to get mad at the store because they don't carry my size — I can either limit my shopping or limit my eating, so I guess I'ma call

Weight Watchers." She sighed heavily and ate the last bite of her key lime pie.

"I hope I didn't hurt your feelings, Alana, because that's the last thing I wanted to do. I wanted to shake off whatever devil has been riding you so you can be happy. And so that fine-azz Roland doesn't go to waste. It's not like we have a bumper crop of tall, rich, handsome, single straight men to pick from, you know. You can't just pass him by, sister."

Alana smiled at Tollie's outspoken frankness and they ended their lunch with laughter and a big hug. She'd had something besides food for lunch; she'd gotten a lot of food for thought. She went back to work and found it was difficult to keep her mind off the things she and Tollie had talked about, or the things she'd listened to, since Tollie had done most of the talking. She decided to leave work early, which meant that she left at five, leaving her assistant manager to lock up, something she also never did. She thought about going over to Adrienne's or to Alexis's but instead of seeking out company, she went home.

She took a shower and put on a pair of pajama pants and an old denim shirt that she used for painting and went to the studio to paint. But her muse had deserted her for the night; she couldn't get started. She'd prepared the palette and brushes and was ready to work on Adrienne's portrait but her hand just wouldn't cooperate.

Forcing herself to add some detailing only resulted in a slight mess that she had to clean up with a rag dampened in linseed oil. It was obviously a fruitless effort so she abandoned it.

She turned off the lights and went to the bathroom to wash her hands, staring in the mirror as she did so. Tollie was right; she did look haggard and wrung-out. Taking a deep breath, she applied more of the expensive eye cream her mother had given her and decided to go to bed.

Standing in the doorway of her bedroom, she looked at the decor with new eyes. Despite what Tollie had said, there were some new things in the room.

The furniture was new, a gift from her mother. An ivory French country queen-size bed with a matching armoire and dresser graced the space, with nightstands on either side of the bed. The duvet and curtains were beautiful, a gift from Adrienne who'd made them from a floral cotton sateen. The chair, in a coordinating color, had been contributed by Aunt BeBe. She'd found it at a yard sale and Alexis had refinished it, painted it and Adrienne had made the cover for the cushions. There was a lot of love in the room and not all of it was from Sam.

But Tollie was right about the portrait.

It was beautifully done, showing him standing against a background of trees and flowers and it was all Sam. His fair skin with the freckles that dusted his face, his curly black hair and green eyes and the smile that was for her eyes only; no one else ever saw that smile. He wasn't a big man, like Roland. He'd been about five-ten, wiry and muscular and full of energy. Her eyes went to the other walls and true enough, there were more pictures of Sam; some had been photographed by Alana and some were her drawings and paintings.

He'd been one of her favorite subjects during their short, happy marriage and she saw no reason not to display them. Why shouldn't they be there? It didn't make the room a shrine, it was just the way she wanted it and if Roland couldn't deal with it, it was his issue, not hers, she thought with a burst of anger.

Surprisingly, she drifted off to sleep. It wasn't a restful sleep; it was fitful and full of dreams. It ended with the worst dream she'd had, ever. She saw Sam, standing at the foot of her bed, his hands in the pockets of his jeans, a familiar and usually endearing pose.

But the expression on his face was totally out of character. He was frowning at her as though she'd done something wrong. He'd never looked at her like that, ever. She sat up and asked him why he was looking at her like that. He shook his head and turned to leave the room without speaking.

Both frightened and angry, she jumped out of bed and went after him, yelling his name over and over.

"Sam, come back here! You can't just walk out on me! What's the matter with you, have you lost your mind? You already left me once and now you have the nerve to leave again without even saying a word to me? What's the matter with you?"

He didn't even turn around, he just kept moving through the house and she chased after him, getting angrier and angrier. Her voice got louder and higher until she was screaming at him, cursing him for all she was worth. She started hurling things at him, anything she could get her hands on.

He started walking to the front door and she knew she had to catch him or she'd never see him again. Her eyes were blurred with tears and she tripped over a low pillowed ottoman which made her fall, but she was close enough to grab his pants leg. His hand was on the doorknob and she tightened her grip. He turned around and said, "Let me go. Let me go, Allie. Let me go."

The sound of her own moaning woke her; she jerked awake and threw off the covers. Her head moved back and forth as she tried to remember where she was. She fully expected to be in the living room by the door, but she was in bed. She was both hot and cold and sopping wet from sweat. Her hair was soaking wet, and so was the pillow and the sheets.

Rubbing her eyes, she realized that she'd been crying. She touched her throat, which was sore and scratchy like she'd been screaming at the top of her lungs. Swinging her legs over the side of the bed, she felt her heart pounding as she tried to stand. Staggering slightly, she made it down the hall to the dining room, looking out into the living room, fully expecting to see the things that she'd hurled at Sam all over the floor, but everything was as she'd left it, as neat as a pin. All she could do was sink into the nearest chair and cry.

She was shivering all over from the clammy sweat on her skin and her heart was still pounding. Tollie was right, she needed to sleep. Suddenly she remembered the prescription she'd been carrying around; her doctor had given her a script for a sleeping aid but she hated taking pills of any kind. But she knew she couldn't go on like this, especially after the horrible dream she'd just had.

Moving quickly, before she changed her mind, she went to the bedroom and put a sweatshirt on over her tank top. She didn't even bother to put on jeans; she just put on a pair of sneakers and tied her hair up in a scarf. In minutes she was headed out.

Wal-mart was open all night and she could get the sleeping pills there.

She stopped at a red light and something moved in her peripheral vision. It was a little dog, obviously lost and frantic. The poor little thing was going from car to car, standing on its hind legs every time it got to a stopped car and it looked utterly pathetic. Without thinking about what she was doing, Alana opened her car door and got out, calling to the poor pup. It heard her soothing voice and came right to her, narrowly missing getting hit by a car. She scooped it up, ignoring the horns honking and the rather uncomplimentary things that a couple of men were shouting at her. She was back behind the wheel in seconds with the wet, bedraggled little dog clinging to her in gratitude. Putting all thoughts of the sleeping pills out of her head, she headed for home.

"You poor baby," she soothed as she drove. "It's okay, I'll take care of you, yes I will. You poor little thing," she crooned. The little dog was panting happily and licking her arm and her hand, whatever it could get to. When she got home she put her new charge inside her jacket and carried it into the house. She kicked off her sneakers at the door and went to the linen closet for some towels to dry the dog.

"You're a girl," she murmured. "You sure are a mess," she said as she rubbed it all over, searching for any wounds or injuries. The dog was mostly white with back markings, especially on its face. It looked like it was wearing a mask; its bright eyes were surrounded by black and its ears, which were enormous, were also black. It was a small dog, about ten or twelve pounds, she guessed, and had what would undoubtedly be silky hair when it was shampooed and groomed. She was extremely friendly, or at least extremely grateful to be out of the cold rainy night. She had plopped herself in Alana's lap and attempted to lick every bit of skin she could get to.

"I'll bet you're hungry," Alana said. "Let's go find you something to eat."

About an hour later, Alana and her new friend were sound asleep on the floor in front of the fireplace. Alana had found a petite filet mignon in the refrigerator and cooked it for the puppy, trimming off every speck of fat and cutting it into bite-sized morsels.

After the puppy ate, she was dry and disheveled, although cute as she could be. Her big eyes stayed glued to Alana and she followed her everywhere as if she thought her new friend would leave her and she'd be out in the cold and rain again.

"Don't worry, sweetie. You're going to be just fine," Alana assured her. She made a makeshift bed of pillows and cushions on the floor and they cuddled up and went to sleep. It was the best sleep Alana had had in years.

A week later, Alana was in her office working on the weekly payroll when the intercom buzzed and she was told that a Mr. Casey wanted to see her. She frowned slightly and said, "Send him back, please."

She looked up as his large body filled the doorway. It was the first time she'd seen him since the night of the party and he looked just as good now as he had then. And he was bearing gifts, as usual: a bunch of her favorite flowers, this time in a gorgeous pink color. She was trying to think of the appropriate greeting but it wasn't needed. His eyes crinkled in a smile as he noticed her companion, who was peering at him from the play area Alana had set up for her.

"Who is this? Where did you come from, cutie?"

"I found her a week ago," Alana informed him.

To her surprise, Roland squatted down and held his fingers out to Domino, who wasted no time in trotting over to meet him. She stood up and put her paws on his knee, staring up at him as though he were the most wonderful thing she'd ever seen in her life. Her plumy tail was wagging so fast that it was a blur of black and white, and she smiled at him for all she was worth.

"Aww, man, she's a sweet little thing, isn't she?" He was so absorbed in making her acquaintance that he'd obviously forgotten why he'd come. He practically tossed the bouquet at Alana and said, "These are for you," in an offhand manner while he and Domino flirted with each other. He finally picked her up in one big hand and sat down with her in his lap. She was shameless, standing up and putting her paws on his broad chest while she tried to give him kisses. He leaned down so she could have her way with his chin and he laughed his appreciation.

"You found her?"

"Yes, I did. I was on my way to the drugstore in the middle of the night and there she was. I couldn't leave the poor little thing."

The morning after she'd found Domino, she'd taken her straight to the vet used by Alexis and Sherri for their dogs and had her checked out thoroughly. The vet said she was less than a year old, and she gave her the basic shots and checked her for a microchip. There was no chip in her, but she'd already been spayed. Alana then took her to the groomer, and when they were finished with her she was even cuter.

Alana had used her time while Domino was being groomed to purchase a dog bed, dog food, leash, collar, harness, toys and a couple of sweaters. And a snappy red raincoat with polka dots for rainy days.

"She's a little charmer, isn't she? Isn't she a papillon?"

"Yes, she is," Alana said, impressed that

he knew the breed. "I put an ad in the paper and I've been watching the ads to see if anyone is looking for her. I really pray no one is because I've gotten really attached to her. I named her Domino."

"Because of her mask, right? She looks like she has on one of those fancy masks that people wear at masquerade balls."

Alana had to smile at the picture Roland made with the little dog in his lap. Domino was generally shy around men, Alana had learned, but she was obviously crazy about Roland. She looked so pleased with herself and so happy to have all his attention that it was just the cutest thing ever. She finally remembered her manners and thanked Roland for the tulips.

"They're lovely. I really appreciate them, Roland."

"I'm glad you like them. I enjoy giving you flowers because I love seeing you happy," he said. "I also brought them as an apology because I think you misunderstood my intent the last time we were together and I want to put things back in order."

"You don't beat around the bush, do you? I guess I should apologize for not taking your calls. That's childish as well as being passive-aggressive and I'm better than that. Do you want a lint roller for your suit?"

He was wearing a really expensive one that looked like it was hand-tailored for his height. It was a beautiful black worsted worn with a lavender shirt and purple silk tie and pocket square that gave him the look of a Fortune 100 CEO.

"Naw, I had some meetings earlier but I'm going home after this, so it's not a problem. I've had dogs all my life so I'm used to dog hair, muddy footprints, whatever. She looks very well cared for, by the way."

"She is. She's been to the vet and the groomer and she has a nice bed and lots of toys and she's the best company in the world. I haven't gotten any answers to my ad and I haven't seen any lost dog posters, and if I do, I don't how I'll react. I don't want to lose her," Alana admitted.

"Don't worry about it, Alana. I think she was meant for you and you were meant for her. It'll be fine." He laughed as Domino gave a little bark of agreement.

"Listen, honey, I had to go out of town and I'm just getting back, which is why I haven't been here to plead my case in person until now. I wanted to know if you'd have dinner with me so we can talk about me putting my foot in my mouth the last time we were together. Does that sound doable?"

Alana felt the usual rush of pleasure she felt whenever Roland was near. "Yes, it does. Would you like to come over tonight? I'm not a trained chef like you, but I can make a mean sloppy joe," she said with a laugh.

"How about if I come to your house and cook for you and Domino? I have the feeling that you don't like leaving her too much."

"You're right about that. The first time I was leaving to go to work she went and got her leash and brought it to me as if to say, 'I'm ready, let's go,' so I've been bringing her in with me. Dinner at home sounds like heaven, actually, and we'd love it. By the way, would you like to see the progress we've made on Black Beauty?"

"Absolutely, I sure would. May I bring the little princess with me?"

"Of course, just don't put her down. She's getting to be real sociable and I don't want her trampled underfoot." She got up and came around the desk. "Come with me and see if you notice any improvements," she said cheerfully.

They walked through the showroom to the service area, stopping several times so that customers could admire Domino. The admiration in the women's eyes for Roland was plain to see, although the men only had eyes for Alana. Tollie came out of the employee break room in time to see the three of them and she was positively jubilant, although she tried to be low-key about it.

"Ooh, there's something so adorable about seeing a great big man with an itty-bitty dog," she said. "It's like seeing a little kid with a great big dog, you know? It's just so cute. I think Miss Domino likes you," she told Roland.

Alana laughed. "She loves him, Tollie. Absolutely adores him. I don't know how I'm going to tear her away from him. It's a good thing he's coming over to cook dinner for us tonight because I don't think she'd forgive me if she didn't see him again."

Roland held Domino up to eye level and said, "She loves her mommy best, you'd better believe it. And she's going to see lots of me, aren't you, baby girl?"

While he and Domino were making kissy faces at each other, Tollie was giving Alana the high sign for getting back on track with Roland. She did a good job of restraining herself because Alana knew she wanted to break into a happy dance.

Tollie went on her way and they continued to the service area where Black Beauty awaited. Roland was speechless when he saw the car. He just stared at it and it was hard to read his reaction. It was stripped of all paint, the tires were off and there were no headlights. But the windows had been installed, the warped and broken axles had been replaced, the grill was brand-new and the frame had been reengineered. The seats were still out of the car, but the new covers were scheduled to be done next.

Assuming that his silence was a form of horror, Alana began to explain to him everything that had been done to the car so far, as well as giving him the order in which the other repairs would be performed.

"We have excellent suppliers and we're waiting for the right head- and taillights, which should be in tomorrow. You'll notice that the chrome has been removed because it's been sent out for replating. The biggest thing was replacing the axles and reworking the frame, which has already been done, and the windows have been put in. The interior wasn't too badly damaged, but since the driver's side had to be replaced, we went ahead and did the whole interior. The specs for this model called for vinyl, but I had some genuine Corinthian leather which I felt you would appreciate. As far as the seats are concerned, the driver's side was damaged so we're replacing both the front and back. We can do them to factory spec for the 1967 model, or we can tweak the design a little to make it custom for you. If you come with me I can show you what I mean."

She was about to lead the way to the upholstery room when Roland grabbed her upper arm and pulled her in for a long, lingering kiss.

"Wow," she gasped. "That was pleasantly unexpected. What was it for?"

"You continue to astound me with everything you do," Roland told her before laying another juicy kiss on her willing lips. Domino yipped indignantly, as if to say that she didn't appreciate sharing the nice man with her mommy.

"I had no idea you'd get so far with it so soon. I can already see that it's going to be a masterpiece. It will look just like it did when it rolled off the line in Detroit, Alana. Damn, girl, you have a master crew here. This is just one of the reasons I love you so much."

Alana's face was deep burgundy from surprise and arousal and she wanted to get him out of the service bay and away from the mechanics who were whistling and clapping to her chagrin. "This way, Roland. Now, please!"

They were alone in the large room and

Alana cleared her throat and tried to go back into automotive professional mode but Roland wasn't interested. He was so hyped up about seeing how much progress had been made on Black Beauty that all he wanted to do was shower her with praise and kisses.

"Roland, I'm trying to show you the computer that makes the patterns and the machine that does the stitching and I need to get your approval on the final design," she said breathlessly. "That takes concentration and you're not paying attention."

"I'm just excited, honey, that's all. As far as the rest of it, I trust you completely. Now come on over here and let me thank you again."

"No, I don't trust you."

"You don't trust me?" He took a step towards her and she barricaded herself behind a huge sewing table.

"You stay right there, mister. We have business to conduct," she reminded him.

He placed Domino on the table and she ran around in happy little circles. "We can mix business and pleasure," he said persuasively.

"Nooo, we can't. Since you can't behave yourself, why don't you go do whatever it is you were going to do and we'll see you tonight," she said firmly.

For a tall man he was certainly nimble because in seconds he'd gotten around the table and had her in his arms. He kissed her one more time and she felt totally scorched by the intensity of his mouth and tongue on hers. Domino barked a few times to express her opinion of the proceedings and Roland and Alana both had to laugh. She looked so indignant standing on the table that he scooped her up again and she gave a little yip of contentment.

"That is going to be one spoiled little girl if I don't keep her on a short leash," Alana said fondly.

"Don't worry about it, honey. I happen to be a very good trainer. I'll show you how to get her trained, starting tonight. How does seven sound?"

"It sounds fine. Do I need to pick up anything for dinner?"

Roland looked surprised at the question. "Of course not. I'm a full-service man. All you have to do is enjoy it."

As they headed back to her office, Alana had a feeling that she was in for a wonderful night.

As Roland handed Domino back to her, he kissed her on the cheek and said he'd see them at seven. Domino whined as he left the office and Alana gave her a nuzzle on the top of her silky head.

"Just remember, chick, he's coming to see both of us. You have to share him, okay?" Domino sighed and licked her on the chin as if to say she'd try but she wasn't making any promises that she couldn't keep.

CHAPTER 7

Alana dashed home after work, once again leaving on time instead of staying late. She wanted to shower and change before Roland came over.

She also wanted to take Domino for a run before dinner. She'd done a good bit of research after finding out her breed, and she was trying to do her best to make sure that her new friend enjoyed good health. Papillons, despite their small size, were very energetic and required a lot of exercise. Alana's house sat on a nice lot with a good-sized backyard, but it would have to be fenced in before it was a suitable place for Domino to run. So for now, they made do with running in the neighborhood. They both got a good workout, so it was a win-win.

Domino continued her workout by running around the house chasing the hard rubber balls Alana had given her; it was a daily activity now. While she careened around, Alana took a quick shower and put on something comfortable but alluring, or so she hoped. She had no idea what was appropriate for datewear these days; the last man she'd dated was Sam.

She chose a casual outfit of Capri leggings in a pretty shade of green and a matching top with a boat neck and ballet sleeves. Her hair was worn loose with her new bangs; she'd gotten them restyled to emulate the First Lady and was quite pleased with the results.

After putting on gold hoop earrings and three gold bangles, she added a spray of Jo Malone eau de toilette and she was ready, except for her shoes. She found one of her ballet flats in the closet, but the other one was missing. She found it rather quickly when Domino poked her head in the door with the missing shoe in her mouth.

"Domino, no, no, no! We don't eat shoes," she said frantically. She moved towards her and Domino gave her a cheeky grin and took off running with her prize.

She was chasing her through the house when the doorbell rang, signaling Roland's arrival. When she greeted him at the door she was slightly out of breath and wearing one shoe.

"Is that a new fashion statement?" he asked with a smile.

Hearing his voice, Domino came running, still carrying the shoe. She was so excited to see Roland that she dropped the shoe and stood on her hind legs to dance around for him. Alana grabbed the shoe and examined it for damage.

"These were my favorites," she said reproachfully. "Aren't you ashamed of yourself?" The gold leather flats had a design of tiny gold studs on the toe. They also had a design of tiny tooth marks, but the leather wasn't torn. "You should be ashamed of yourself, little girl. I don't chew on your things, do I?"

Roland laughed all the way to the kitchen where he put down the bags he was carrying. He had three canvas tote bags full of provisions for their meal. Once he put them on the work island, he turned to Alana and cupped her face in his big warm hands to give her a kiss.

"Don't worry about it, honey. Her training starts tonight. You just have to let her know who's boss. Give her the right cues and she'll stay within the boundaries you set for her, you'll see."

Alana took his coat so she could hang it up, pausing to admire him for a moment.

He was dressed in what were undoubtedly well-loved jeans, to judge from their worn appearance and the way they fit his long muscular legs. With it he had on a heavy off-white cotton baseball jersey with the long sleeves pushed up to show off his forearms.

Whether he was dressed up or dressed down, Roland was one of the best-looking men she'd ever seen. She put his coat away and came back in the kitchen to find him washing his hands with Domino stationed next to him watching every move. Roland put on a big white apron after he dried his hands and began preparing his work space.

"Can I help?" Alana asked.

"You can watch," Roland told her. "I'm doing this for you. If you help it'll take the fun out of it for me."

Touched, Alana asked if he wanted something to drink.

"A little wine would be nice. And a little music."

Soon she was sitting on a stool, watching Roland assemble a meal that made her mouth water. They were both sipping white wine while he boned chicken thighs and sliced mushrooms, shallots, black olives and celery. He browned the chicken in olive oil and a bit of butter, and then caramelized the vegetables. Everything went into a cast-iron casserole dish except the olives. He poured some white wine into the skillet and deglazed it before pouring it over the chicken and vegetables.

It went into the oven to braise and he set about making risotto with fresh baby peas and sautéed spinach with bacon and chopped pistachios.

"Did you always want to be a chef?" Alana asked.

"Not really. I didn't have a real passion for it the way Jared does, or like Lucas and Damon. I run the business side of things, but I wanted to know what I was doing, so I went to culinary school in New York and then I developed a real love for cooking. I still didn't want to run a kitchen in a restaurant. I can, but I like teaching better. I like showing kids that they can have a future doing something creative, artistic and lucrative. I also like feeding people."

"If this tastes as good as it smells, you're doing a wonderful job. I think Domino wants some already."

Sure enough, the little dog was spinning around on her hind legs, hoping for a handout. But Roland had a better idea.

"The worst thing you can do is give them people food. They develop a taste for it and they won't eat their own food, for one thing. And for another, it's bad for them. Too many sugars and fats and it can give them pancreatitis, kidney disease, tooth decay, all kinds of things," he said as he began mixing some things in a bowl.

Alana was impressed. "How do you know so much about dogs?"

"My granddad, the one who gave me Black Beauty, used to raise dogs and train them. He knew everything there was to know about dogs. Including this recipe for dog biscuits," he said as he began rolling out the stiff dough and cutting it into small strips. He put them on a cookie sheet and slipped them in the oven after adding the olives to the casserole. "These are better than anything you can buy for her and she'll love them. By the way, if you do give her a little extra in her food, make sure it's beef or lamb. Small dogs like that often have an allergy to chicken and other poultry and it makes their feet itch, so watch out for that."

"You're an amazing guy, Roland. Is there anything you don't know about?" Alana said with her brilliant smile.

"Yeah, actually there is. I don't know how to express myself properly when I'm discussing something of extreme importance with someone who means the world to me," he said. "I was trying to explain something to you when I left that night and I didn't do it very well. I know I confused you and hurt your feelings and that's the last thing I want to do in this life." He looked at her, lovingly and sincerely, and she felt humbled by his words.

"Roland, thank you for saying that, but I think I should apologize, too. I didn't realize it, but a friend of mine helped me understand some things the other day." She looked reflective as she went on. "I have three sisters, a very savvy mom and an aunt who's just amazing and I'm very close to all of them. But it took a non-relative — it took a friend to make me see the light. Why is that?"

"That's a good question, Alana. I think because our relatives are too close to our situation to be objective. They want to protect us so much that it's difficult for them to give that tough love, or whatever they call it these days." He glanced at the timer and took out the dog biscuits, putting them on the counter to cool. "I'm going to set the table and when I'm finished, the meal will be ready for your consumption and, I hope, your approval."

One of the tote bags contained plates, a tablecloth, silverware and other accoutrements. True to his word, Roland had the table looking gorgeous right down to candles and flowers. In a few minutes they were seated with plates of truly appetizing food in front of them.

After saying grace together, Alana daintily dug in and the explosion of flavors in her mouth made her eyes close and she had to hold back a deep moan. She concentrated completely on the food with a minimum of conversation. When her plate was almost clean, she finally gave her personal chef her full attention.

"Roland, this was perfect. Absolutely delicious," she said with a sigh of utter delight. "I can't remember when I enjoyed anything as much as this. Thank you so much. And Domino thanks you, too," she added.

Domino was at his feet, still happily gnawing on her homemade treat.

"I've got dessert for you, too. Not right this second, I can tell you're quite replete at the moment. Why don't you go get comfortable while I clean up the kitchen," he suggested. He could see that she was about to protest and he took her hand, kissing her fingertips. "Don't even try it. This is something I have in common with the VanBurens and my step-dad. No lady lifts a finger when I'm around. Except my sisters, they're on their own," he laughed.

Alana leaned over and kissed him. "I'm not going to argue with you. I'm going to take the little princess out for her nighttime stroll while you do what you insist upon doing. I'm very lucky because she appears to be totally housebroken, but I'm trying to keep her on a tight schedule."

Roland's face showed immediate conflict. "How far are you going? I'll go with you. I don't like the idea of you walking around at night with just a teeny-tiny dog for protection."

"We're going out in the backyard. It's very well-lit. I need to get it fenced so it's safe for her to play back there. She needs lots of exercise, which came as a surprise. She races through here like her tail is on fire at least three times a day," Alana said. "Go get your leash, sweetie, we're going outside."

Roland watched them through the big kitchen window as he dispatched what little cleaning there was to be done. While he was attending to that and keeping his eye on his two ladies, the house phone in the kitchen rang. It went to the answering machine and he heard a woman's voice. "I'm answering your ad in the paper about finding a dog. I think it's mine. My name is . . ."

He grabbed the phone at once. "Hello?

Hello? . . . No, I didn't place the ad, my fiancée did. . . . How about we meet tomorrow? What time is good for you? . . . Great, that's fine. Eleven sounds fine, I'll see you then."

This was just what Alana was afraid of, someone coming forward with a claim on Domino. One thing was definitely sure; he wasn't going to spoil their evening. He'd deal with it tomorrow.

Alana couldn't remember a more relaxing evening. After she walked Domino around the yard, they went to the family room and lit the fireplace. That is, Alana went to the family room and Domino went to find Roland. When the two of them came in the comfortable large room, the big flat-screen was on, tuned to Netflix, and a stack of DVDs was on the coffee table awaiting Roland's perusal. Alana was sitting in the corner of the sofa with a pillow in her lap.

"Come and stretch out. You've earned it," she said with a smile.

He kicked off his shoes and lay down with his head in her lap, moaning with pleasure as she leaned over to kiss him. The moan turned into a groan as Domino jumped on his stomach. She ran up his chest to give him a few kisses of her own. Finally she settled down possessively, keeping a keen eye on Alana to make sure that she got her fair share of smooches.

"I told her that we have to share you, but I think she plans on phasing me out," Alana said wryly. "She's staked a claim on you and I'm pretty sure I'm getting kicked to the curb."

"Never going to happen in a million years, honey. We'll have to get her a boyfriend of her own because I'm already spoken for." Roland's eyes were closed and he looked completely content.

"Ha! I knew it — there's no way that a handsome, personable man who can cook and understands women is single. Who is she and is she coming after me?" Alana demanded. She started giggling madly as Roland managed to tickle her from his supine position. Domino forgot that she was infatuated with Roland and came out on the side of Team Mommy, whining and barking at Roland anxiously.

"I'm sorry, sweetie. We were just playing," Alana said soothingly. Domino walked right over Roland's face to get to Alana, her body language clearly showing her concern.

"Aughh! See how you do me? After I made you cookies and everything," he grumbled.

He sat up and put his arms around Alana, kissing her on the cheek. "We were playing, baby girl. Don't get upset." He held a finger out to her and she looked at it suspiciously before snuggling closer to Alana.

"Wow. I think I've been shut down permanently," Roland said with a smile.

"She'll be fine in a minute, I'm sure. Maybe she came from an abusive home or something. Do you want to watch a movie?"

"You can turn it on, but it'll be background noise. What I really want to do is finish our earlier conversation because I don't want there to be any more misunderstandings between us. We've got something really special here and I don't want to mess it up, Alana."

She didn't say anything and Roland turned her face to his to make sure she was giving him her full attention.

"Are you still with me, honey?"

"Yes, of course I am. And yes," she said slowly, "I think this is something special, Roland. I haven't even looked at another man since Sam died. It was such a horrible mess and I was so crushed by the whole thing that finding love again was the last thing on my mind. After the trial, I just shut down. I mean I shut that part of myself down and I was never going to open it again."

"The trial? They caught the guy?"

"Yes, they did. And I had to go to court and testify and it was just awful. I wanted him put away forever, of course, and so did Sam's family. But I always had the feeling that the Dumonds blamed me for his death. They were really cold to me afterwards. They barely spoke to me at the funeral and there were some really shitty things said about me after they found out that there was an insurance policy. They were going to come after me in civil court for wrongful death or something but when I gave his mother a pile of money she suddenly changed her mind."

Roland was appalled. "You've really been through it, haven't you, baby? I can understand why you withdrew from relationships. You lived through some truly tragic ordeals. You lost your husband, you lost your baby and you had to deal with the trial and with his family. I know your family was there for you, but that was a tough row to hoe."

"A what? When did you become a Mississippi farm hand?" she teased.

"That's one of my granddad's favorite expressions. He came up to Chicago to work, but he was a Mississippi man through

133

and through, and never forgot where he came from. But don't change the focus here, Alana. You've been through hell, and I can see why you've been holding back. But, honey, nothing like that can happen with us. You can't let that tragedy, or tragedies, dictate the rest of your life."

"You're right," she said quietly.

"I'm what?"

Alana was idly stroking Domino's big butterfly-shaped ears, running her fingers through the long silky hair. If she had looked at him, she would have seen the relief and happiness on his face, but she was concentrating on the little dog.

"You're right, Roland. I was living a half-life of regrets and bad dreams and fear and loss. I'm not going to do that anymore. I want to have a whole life, I want it all. You're the first man I've allowed to get near me since I lost Sam and I don't want to lose whatever it is that we've got going on."

She stopped talking because Roland covered her mouth with his. His tongue teased her lips apart until he gained full access to all the sweetness that was waiting for him. Alana didn't try to resist, she joined in with enthusiasm, returning every stroke of his tongue with hers.

Heat started coursing through her body,

piercing every sensitive spot. Roland moved his hand to begin an intimate exploration of her breasts, but his arm wouldn't move, primarily because Domino had his sleeve in her mouth. She stood up in Alana's lap and looked at the two of them sternly.

"You're not going to be a problem, are you?" Roland retrieved his sleeve from the little dog and gave Alana an affectionate wink. "Have you been letting her sleep with you?"

Alana looked sheepish and admitted that she had.

"Well, that explains it. We're going to break her of that habit tonight."

"Good luck with that. Speaking of habits that need to be broken, did it bother you seeing the portrait of Sam over my bed?" She watched him carefully, waiting for his answer.

"Yes, it did," he admitted.

"It's not there anymore."

Roland's face brightened into a broad smile. "I'd like to see that. Let's get Miss Lady situated and take a tour."

He stood up and whipped off his sweater, revealing a ribbed undershirt that fit nice and snug. Her eyes opened wide and her mouth formed a juicy O of awe-struck admiration. She was already hot from his kiss and the heat grew in intensity until she was pretty sure that Miss Alana was on fire. It was the first time she'd seen a half-naked man since Sam's death and Roland was more than worth the wait. His body was just beautiful; there was no other word for it. His arms were smooth as copper silk and the muscles were perfect. His chest was broad and muscled and as hard as his arms. He smelled fantastic, too; like balsam and cedar and pure male.

Her hand went out to him and before she could stop herself, she was stroking one of his biceps in admiration.

"Wow," she breathed softly.

He smiled rakishly and flexed his muscles to elicit another sigh from Alana. "You like that? How about this," he said, before whipping off the thin undershirt to reveal pecs that were works of art.

Alana was transfixed by what she was seeing. She had to touch him again, just had to. Her small hand stroked his chest and she was amazed to find the skin as warm and supple as satin. He popped his pecs and they moved, making her jump in surprise and giggle, just like Julia Roberts in the iconic scene from Pretty Woman with Richard Gere and the jewelry box. They both laughed until he said, "Is that thing washable? Your top thing, I mean."

"Sure it is. Why?"

"Take it off, honey — we're going to need it."

Puzzled but emboldened by his moves, Alana did as he asked. She crossed her arms and took the hem of the slim-fitting top in her trembling fingers. She slowly pulled it up until the garment was off.

Holding it out to Roland, she was embarrassed but was gratified by his sharp intake of breath. Her perfect breasts were on full display in a coral demi-bra that fastened with a tiny rosebud between the lace cups. It was his turn to reach for her treasures and he did so reverently, stroking the silky exposed skin with a dazed look on his face.

"This is like opening the best gift I ever received," he said. "Come on, let's get her highness situated."

Minutes later, Domino was happily snuggled in her bed with her favorite toy, a soft fuzzy bunny. Roland had put the bed in the guest room across the hall from the master suite and lined it with Alana's green top and his undershirt, using his expensive J. Peterman jersey as a coverlet.

Alana was surprised and pleased when the little dog turned around a few times and settled down with a satisfied sigh and a doggie smile. Her eyes were closed before they left the room. Alana was both touched and impressed by the sight.

"That was so clever," she praised. "I never would've thought of that."

All of Roland's attention was focused on Alana. She moved into the bedroom and was soon sitting in the center of the bed with her legs crossed, looking extremely tempting in her leggings and bra. He glanced around the bedroom and noticed that the pictures on the pale green walls had indeed changed. Sam was no longer glowering at him from above the bed; a large watercolor of the backyard had taken his place. He sat down on the bed and lay back on the pillows with a satisfied smile.

"How did you ever think of putting our clothes in the bed with her? It certainly did the trick."

"If you come over here, I'll tell you," Roland answered.

She promptly scooted over so that he could put his arms around her as she relaxed into his body. He was so warm that she felt like she was in a cocoon. Her hands couldn't stop moving over the smooth planes of his chest. It was an amazing sensation; his body was so hard yet his skin was as soft as the petals of her favorite flower.

She was so engrossed in learning the feel of him that she forgot that she'd asked him a question.

"If she smells us, it gives her comfort," he said. "That's what you do with puppies to get them to sleep when they leave their mother, you put something of yours in the crate and it helps them nod off."

"It helps who do what? What are you talking about, Roland?"

His chest moved as a deep laugh rose and escaped through his throat. "I was telling you how I got Miss Domino to go to sleep, but your mind seems to be on something else."

Alana rose up on one elbow so that she was looking down at him, her free hand continuing to move up and down, her palm tracing his hardened nipples in a slow circular motion. "My mind is totally on you, I'm afraid. I can't seem to think about anything else at the moment. Is that okay with you?"

He moaned from the pleasure she was giving him before answering. "I'm absolutely fine with it." His hands started moving over her, exploring the soft skin of her taut body. When his fingers reached the waistband of her leggings, he paused.

"Take them off," she said in a husky whisper.

Once her shapely legs were bare, Roland looked at them with a potent hunger in his eyes. "I've been meaning to tell you how beautiful your legs are," he said, scorching a heated path down her thighs with his palms. "And I've been wanting to see them just like this, with nothing between us."

"If that's the case, one of us has too many clothes on," Alana replied. "What are you going to do about that?"

Instead of answering, Roland stood up and removed his jeans and briefs. He literally took Alana's breath away. He stood before her totally naked, revealing every inch of his body and he was like nothing she'd ever seen before. Without the covering of his stylish clothes, he was even more beautiful, if such a thing was possible. His broad shoulders and arms were the perfect proportion to his narrow waist and he really did have a six-pack; his abdominal muscles were so defined it was like looking at him through a Hi-Def camera lens.

She made herself take in his muscular thighs and calves before concentrating on his manhood because it took all her attention. Now she understood why heroines in the romance novels Alexis and Adrienne loved were always worried about whether it would fit; Roland was huge and hard and for a fleeting moment she was positive it wasn't going to work. But by golly, she was going to give it her best shot.

"Is everything okay? This is all I have to work with so if you don't like it, we're in trouble," Roland said.

Alana brought herself up to a kneeling position, facing Roland as she reached to unfasten her bra. "Don't be ridiculous," she murmured. "If I didn't want to make love with you so badly I'd be trying to sculpt you. I'm going to tell you something that you can't use against me in any way," she warned him. "You are the most gorgeous man I've ever seen in my life. It's a good thing you're a good man or you'd be really, really dangerous."

His eyes widened and he laughed heartily, but not so hard that he forgot the task at hand. He moved her hands so that he could undo her bra and watch her plump, round breasts come into his view for the first time. They weren't huge; they were just perfect for her size and his desire. Now she was wearing only the tiny thong that matched the bra and she looked better than all the Victoria's Secret Angels put together, as far as Roland was concerned.

She was slender, but her proportions were absolutely perfect. Her dark skin gleamed in the dim light of the room and her scent was intoxicating. She smelled like flowers in a spring rain, with a hint of pure woman that was all her. He tugged at the delicate garment until she was free of it and they were both entirely bare. They went into each other's arms and held on tight, joining their mouths as their naked flesh touched for the first time.

Alana's hips began to move as she sought more of the hot passion that was surging between them. Her hands tightened on his arms as he began to kiss her neck and the sensitive place between her breasts before taking her hardened nipple in his mouth. She gasped and trembled all over at the sensations he created, feelings that were new and wonderful and so much more than she expected. He slowed his movements and pulled away from her, causing her eyes to fill with confusion.

"We only have one first time, baby, and I want it to be right. Come here and let me show you what I mean."

CHAPTER 8

It only took a couple of minutes for the covers to be turned back and Roland began to show Alana exactly what he meant about making their first time special. She was on her back with her knees bent. He was next to her, resting on his elbow so that he could look down at her with an expression she'd never seen on a man's face before, not even Sam's.

Roland leaned down to kiss her again while his hand freely explored the source of the moisture between her legs. His mouth moved down her neck as he tasted her for the first time. He lingered over her breasts, sucking her nipples until she moaned his name, over and over. Her toes were curling and flexing and she could feel the wet heat on his fingers increase as her inner walls pulsed harder. He didn't relent, though. He continued to stroke her, using his moistened thumb to massage her tender spot, the most

sensitive and responsive part of her woman-
hood. He knew the moment her first orgasm
began, not just because of the warm flow
that gushed from her delicate flesh, but the
wild movement of her hips and the con-
tented look of surrender on her face.

Alana's heart was still beating rapidly and
she was breathless. Roland turned so that
he was on his back, bringing Alana with
him. She lay on his chest and they were so
close that he could feel their hearts beating
as one. If he expected moments of quiet
repose he was mistaken and surprised as
Alana kissed him deep and fierce. At the
same time she positioned herself on his
manhood, sliding onto the crown and moving back and forth until their bodies were
joined.

He pushed, gently at first, but the feel of
her, warm and slick, created an urgency that
couldn't be ignored. The kiss was broken as
her mouth opened to let out a sound of pure
passion. She gripped his shoulders, holding
on tight as her hips assumed the rhythm
and she rode Roland, giving him as good as
she was getting.

He couldn't remember ever being this
aroused. The sheen of her dark skin against
his, the love-swollen nipples and the unbridled ecstasy on her face were almost too

much for him. His hands tightened on her hips as the ride continued but when she pulled him in, deeper than he could have believed possible, the sensations they made together began pushing him to the brink. His hands tightened on her slender hips, holding on as he tried to force himself to resist the lure of her tight, taut body.

She drove him harder, her walls squeezing him until the suction was too much and he exploded deep inside her. His voice was raw and hoarse as he ground out her name but the sound of it excited her even more and she continued to slide up and down until she joined him in an incredible climax. Their bodies were trembling and soaked with sweat as she finally collapsed on top of him.

When she could finally speak again, which took several minutes, Alana took a deep breath and murmured, "Wow."

It took Roland a moment longer to answer. "Very wow. Are you okay?"

He could feel the ripples of happiness rise in her body as she giggled softly. "I think that's a slight understatement, but I can assure you that I'm much better than okay. I'm wonderful," she assured him.

She rested her head on his shoulder and looked at their fingers, which were locked together. "That was way better than my dreams, Roland."

It was her turn to feel his chest rumbling as he laughed softly. "Are you saying that you've been dreaming about me? What kind of dreams were you having?"

Alana shifted so that she was supporting her head with her hand and looked at him with a bewitching smile. "Sexy ones. Erotic, romantic, hot and nasty ones. I've dreaming about you ever since Sherri and Lucas's wedding. Are you shocked?"

"Not shocked," he said with his special smile. "I'm surprised, though. I'm surprised that you're telling me about it because most women wouldn't admit it. But I'm not shocked because I've been dreaming about you for months. You've been slipping into my dreams since the day I met you."

She returned his smile and accompanied it with a kiss. "Were they good dreams?"

"They were great, but not as good as this," he said. "I used to wake up hard as a damned rock every morning and then I'd be disappointed because you weren't in the bed with me."

"I'm here now. So which dream do you want to come true?"

Minutes later Alana was in the last place she planned on being; she was standing on her tiptoes in her free-standing glass shower with her arms locked around Roland's waist. They were kissing madly, which was part of many of her dreams, but he was shampooing her hair, which wasn't. Since her hair had been wrecked in the name of love, Roland insisted on shampooing it for her. He'd finger-combed it and when she was wet from head to toe, he'd applied her fragrant Carol's Daughter shampoo and began to distribute it gently but sensually. It felt odd at first, but it was both soothing and arousing.

"Roland, this feels wonderful," she said as she pressed closer to his body. "I think you've done this before."

He laughed as he began to rinse her hair with the handheld shower. "I have, honey. Remember I had an overworked mother and a slew of sisters. There was no money for the hairdresser so I had to pitch in and wash a lot of heads. Only I'd put them on the kitchen counter and wash them in the sink. I didn't use expensive shampoo, either. I used washing powder. Tide works the best," he added.

Alana's eyes flew open. "No, you didn't put detergent in their hair! I don't believe you," she said.

"You're right, I'm lying. But I did do their

hair. I learned how to braid and blow-dry and I even learned how to give relaxers. I had a girlfriend who went to beauty school and she hooked me up."

A totally unexpected pang of an unfamiliar emotion snaked through Alana; it was jealousy, pure and simple. It was ridiculous to feel anything remotely like jealousy about some woman that he probably hadn't laid eyes on in years, but there it was. And there she was being possessive, how crazy was that?

"Well, you learned a lot from her. How can I repay you?"

"You can do mine next time," he said with a grin. They both laughed.

"Since you're bald I'll skip the shampoo, but I give a great massage. Ooh!" she gasped as he finished rinsing her hair and started guiding the handheld shower spray all over her body. He let the water cascade over her breasts before changing the pressure to a pulsing massage. The hard pulsing brought her already sensitive nipples to huge points for Roland to feast on while he plied the spray between her legs. The twin sensations made her knees go weak and he had to abandon the hose in order to hold on to her hips.

"Okay, that's enough for now. I don't want

you to fall," Roland said. He reached over and turned the water off with one hand before wrapping her in a towel off the warming rack. She returned the favor.

"I thought that was an extravagant gift when Aunt BeBe sent it to me for my housewarming, but I love it." She caught a glimpse of herself in the mirror and shook her head. Her relaxed hair stood out in wild spirals, a marked contrast to her previous sleek look.

"I have no more secrets, Roland. You've seen it all now," she said ruefully.

He cupped her face with both hands and kissed her deeply. He pulled her lower lip into his mouth and gently sucked it before teasing her mouth open with his tongue. After a long, satisfying exchange, Roland looked down at Alana and assured her that she was beautiful.

"There's nothing I'd change about you. Nothing," he told her. "Everything about you is just perfect. Your skin, your smile, those dimples, your body and your beautiful hair," he said, running his hands over it.

"You're very sweet, but I dare you to run your fingers through it," Alana said with a sigh. "You'll cut your fingers on this stuff."

Roland picked her up, carried her to the bedroom and dropped her on the bed, making her laugh aloud. "Don't be disparaging the woman of my dreams," he said in a mock-fierce tone. "You forget that I already knew every inch of you before I touched you. When I saw you the first time at Alexis's crazy party that Jared and I drove all night to get to, I knew. You were sitting on the floor playing with the puppies he brought her and I knew. And I started having dreams about you and I saw you exactly as you are and I knew I was right. Everything about you is just the way I knew it would be, so talk what you know," he said, removing his towel.

"You're more than I expected," she said demurely. "My dreams were very detailed and specific, but there are some things for which your subconscious can't prepare you. But those things are very nice surprises — stupendous, huge surprises, as a matter of fact." She lowered her eyes to his most potent attribute and smiled. "Get comfortable so I can make another dream come true. Lie on your stomach," she said, turning to the dresser for a spray bottle of Moroccan oil.

She removed her towel and straddled his long body, spraying the lightly scented oil over his magnificent back and shoulders. While stroking and kneading until he moaned with pleasure, she talked to him in a soft, dreamy voice that drove Roland crazy.

"I've done this to you before," she murmured. "Lots of times. We've made love so many times in so many places, at least in my dreams."

"We'll make love so many times you won't be able to remember them all," he vowed. "And it'll all be real." His words stopped because she'd reached his butt and the feel of her hands on his ass was driving him crazy. Sounds of pleasure were the only sound in the room while she treated his thighs and calves in the same way, all the way down to his feet. When he felt her supple fingers on his feet, he turned over quickly.

"I'm sorry, Alana, but my feet are extremely ticklish," he confessed. "It's my one weakness."

"Everybody's entitled to one," she said. "But as long as you've turned over, let's do this side."

She began working her magic again but it was much more intense because she used more than her hands on his nipples. She was once again astride him as her hands smoothed the delicate oil up and down his chest and stomach. He shuddered as her mouth surrounded the hypersensitive skin of his flat nipple, heating his flesh as she breathed on it, and then licked it like it was her favorite candy. She teased it gently with her teeth and sucked hard, creating a sensation like heat lightning flashing all over his body.

She treated the other side to the same delight before licking him down to his navel. When her tongue plundered the little cavern he felt like he was levitating off the bed. It was a shock to find out how responsive that part of his body was, but he didn't have time to dwell on it because she continued her exploration.

By now Roland was totally mesmerized. He watched her through half-closed eyes and the sight was arousing, amazing and humbling. The way her cocoa skin looked in the dim light, the wild curls floating around her face and the pure sensuality she exuded combined in an explosion of passion that could have been another of his nightly visions. When she cupped him and put her soft, luscious lips around the crown of his manhood it snapped him back to reality.

This was as real as it could get.

She licked him up and down, swirling her tongue around the tip before treating every inch of his heavy length to the same delight until he reached the point of no return. A low growl came from deep inside as he swiftly changed positions so that she was in the receiving position and he was the giver.

He buried his face between her thighs and began to devour the sweet nectar that gushed from her, exploring every bit of her secret treasure until his tongue found the source of her magic. He licked and sucked until he could feel every throbbing pulse that let him know she was exploding from the pleasure he was giving her. She was trembling and her hips were moving to get more of what he was giving her, and he continued on his quest to satisfy her like no man ever had.

When he knew she'd come again, he kept on until her cries of passion filled the bedroom. He finally relented, reluctantly slowing his pace and kissing his way up her shaking body until their mouths met and locked and they could taste their elixir on each other's tongues.

If there was anything else more profoundly sensual that could happen between a man and woman, he had no idea what it could be. After a series of long, amazing kisses, they finally fell asleep and he held her all night long.

■ ■ ■ ■

Alana was blissfully asleep, basking in the warm bed and enjoying a restful slumber without a single dream. A wet kiss on her cheek dragged her back to consciousness, but she didn't open her eyes, she couldn't; it just felt too good to be where she was.

Another lick followed, which made her stifle a laugh. Then something small, cold and wet touched her neck and her eyes flew open. Domino was next to her on the pillow wearing her most winsome smile. Actually, she looked like she was laughing.

"How did you get in here, little girl? What have you been up to while I was sleeping?" Alana yawned and put her hand up to smooth her hair away from her face, cringing as she felt the tangled mess that now crowned her head.

"I let her in here because she was wondering where you were. We've been up for a long time, honey. I had a shower and got dressed, then took her for a walk. After that, I made you breakfast. We've been very productive while you were sleeping." Roland sounded both amused and affectionate and he looked way too good. He was indeed dressed, but in different clothes.

Alana sat up, pulling the sheet up with her. "You're way too handsome, I hope you realize that. You make me feel like a true hag and it's so unfair. Did you go home and change clothes or something?"

Roland shook his head and tried not to let his smile show. She had no idea how adorably sexy she was with no makeup, her wild mass of curls and no clothes. Especially the no clothes part.

He walked over to the bed and sat next to her, which gave Domino a thrill, as she ran to jump in his lap. From her wary expression, Alana was less thrilled. She pulled the sheet up over her mouth while he answered her question.

"No, I didn't go anywhere. I always have some clean clothes in the car because in the restaurant business you never know what could happen. You might have to work a double or triple shift. You might wreck a shirt or whatever. I'm always prepared for any disaster because I'm kind of particular about my appearance."

"I hadn't noticed," Alana mumbled. "I need to get up and brush my teeth and things, so why don't you and your girlfriend give me a little privacy?"

"What could you possibly be hiding from me at this point? There are no secrets between us anymore," he said with a satisfied smirk.

"I can sterilize cattle with my morning breath, so unless you want a sample, I'd get out of here."

"Liar. I smelled your breath this morning when I kissed you and it was just as sweet as you are. And by the way, I've never seen a woman who looks as cute as you do first thing in the morning, so we're not gonna have that conversation again. I'll leave, but only so I can set the table for you. Breakfast is served as soon as you're ready. C'mon, sugar-pup, let's leave Mommy alone so she can have some privacy."

It didn't take Alana long to shower and dress, especially since despite the grouchy face she'd given to Roland, she was in a fabulous mood. She sang in the shower and hummed as she slathered her body with lotion and body cream, finishing up with a generous spray of eau de parfum.

Her hair was a hot mess, but she could always go to Sanctuary, Alexis's salon/spa. For now she slipped into her normal work clothes, jeans and a teal long-sleeved polo shirt with the Custom Classics logo. She applied her usual workday makeup, which consisted of a tinted moisturizer, a little blush and a couple of coats of mascara.

She pulled her damp hair up into a ponytail and tied a scarf around the elastic band. It was an Afro-puff; there was no getting around it. Maybe people would think it was retro, she thought as she added some gold hoop earrings.

As promised, breakfast was waiting for her. Roland had sliced a banana, covered it with her favorite pineapple Greek yogurt, drizzled it with honey and cinnamon and sprinkled it with granola. There was also piping-hot coffee and a muffin that he'd obviously made from scratch since she had no packaged mixes in her pantry.

Her heart was filled with happiness and gratitude. He pulled out her chair and gave her a sweet kiss. Domino was busy with one of her dog biscuits, but she carried it over to Alana and sat down at her feet while she devoured it. Everything was happy, domestic and peaceful, almost too much so. Alana sipped her coffee and took a bite of the muffin, which melted in her mouth. It was also banana, with the addition of chopped walnuts and it tasted like heaven.

"Roland, thank you so much for this. This is a wonderful breakfast," she said. She took a good long look at him, looking relaxed, sexy and totally at home. Without thinking about what she was saying, she blurted out what was on her mind.

"Why aren't you married? How is it that a tall, beautiful man with a great personality, incredible sex appeal and mad kitchen skills is walking around unattached? Or are you hiding a wife and six children somewhere that I should know about," she muttered as she took a spoonful of yogurt.

He laughed before taking a sip of his coffee. "I'm not married because I was taking my time. I had my birth father as a horrible example of how not to behave in a marriage and I was determined to take my time and do it right. I plan on getting married one time and one time only. Marriage is serious business and after what my mother went through I wasn't sure I wanted to do it at all. My granddad, her father, was a great role model for me — he was married to my grandmother until the day she made her transition and he never looked at another woman, ever."

"He sounds like a great man," Alana said thoughtfully. "So you've never had a serious girlfriend, never been engaged or anything? How could the women in Chicago miss a man like you?"

"Who says they did?" Roland teased her. "I will be more than glad to share my checkered past with you anytime, but I have a couple of appointments this morning. How about we take this up later tonight? Dinner, dancing, bungee-jumping, parasailing, whatever you like," he said with the smile that made her heart rate accelerate every time she saw it.

"Sounds like the plan of a crazy man," she answered. "Call me later and we'll decide. Thanks again for this," she said, indicating the pretty place setting.

He kissed her again, but this time was longer and sweeter and tasted like the excellent coffee he'd brewed. "Talk to you later."

Domino scrambled to her feet as she realized that her hero was leaving. He scratched her between her ears and assured her that he'd be back later. Both she and Alana stared at the door after he left.

With a deep and heartfelt sigh, she polished off her meal, cleared the table and put the dishes in the dishwasher. If every day could start like this one, it would be a wonderful life.

"Let's go, sweetie. Time for work," she said cheerfully, and Domino ran to get her leash.

Roland was still overwhelmed by his night with Alana, so much so that it was difficult for him to focus on the task at hand. He went to the drive-thru window at his bank and made a withdrawal, but his mind was still on Alana. He wished with all his heart that they were still in bed because there was no place else that he wanted to be, but he was on a mission.

Even as he drove to his first appointment, he couldn't stop thinking about the amazing woman he'd held all night. He'd always known that she was smart, successful and intelligent, but nothing had really prepared him for the depth of her passion. A slight tremor of memory passed through him as he recalled their lovemaking in great detail. He'd been prepared for her sensuality, but she'd exceeded every expectation. It was actually hard for him to keep driving because all he wanted to do was go get his woman and take her right back home to pick up where they'd left off.

He almost missed his turn because his mind was filled with images of his beautiful goddess and her siren's charms.

His destination was the law office of Royce Griffin. He'd met Royce when Sherri and Lucas got married; he'd been one of the groomsmen, as a matter of fact. Royce was a funny, down-to-earth guy as well as being a very skilled attorney. While Alana was still asleep, he'd called Royce to ask for a favor which he was happy to grant. He had drawn up a contract to handle Roland's request and he was here to pick it up. He located the building with no problem and entered Royce's office, which was a bit eclectic, to say the least.

Everything about the place looked like Royce; it was spotlessly clean and furnished in an artsy, bohemian style that reflected the personality of the owner. He was amused by the large bird in the brass cage in the reception area.

"Client! Client! Get out here, don't keep him waiting!" the bird squawked.

Royce stuck his head out of his private office and waved Roland in. "That's Thelonius, my alarm system, intercom and part-time receptionist. My secretary had to run to the courthouse, so he's earning his sunflower seeds," he chuckled. "C'mon in, man, it's all done."

The pristine reception area gave way to organized chaos in Royce's office. There were stacks of files on every level surface, including the desk and one of the chairs in front of the desk. "I need a bigger place in the worst way, but it's on my to-do list. This building is old and in need of serious remodeling, but the price is right, so I stick around."

Roland looked at the office with great interest since real estate was his sideline. "You know, I might have a few ideas to run by you about this place. We'll have to get together and talk about it soon. Meanwhile, thanks a lot for doing this, man. I really appreciate you being able to draw it up with basically no advance notice."

"No problem, man, I'm sure it'll cover all your bases, but if you need anything else just let me know. You should be good, though."

The two men chatted a bit more and Royce told Roland he'd send him a bill for his services. Thanking him again, Roland left for his next appointment, a far more important one. It didn't take him long to locate the Starbucks and park his truck. He went inside and looked around for the person with whom he had a critical meeting. He was still standing near the door, scanning the customers, when a woman approached him.

"Are you the man I talked to last night about the dog?"

She was medium height, superficially attractive with perfectly applied makeup and long auburn hair that he had no reason to believe was hers by nature. Her figure was spectacular, if you were excited about seeing a 44DD crammed into a 42C, or the sight of a middle-aged woman wearing skin-tight leggings that were at least one size too small, squishing her chubby legs down to her thick ankles teetering on Lucite-soled platform shoes. Roland wasn't, but this wasn't a date, it was a business transaction.

"Yes, I'm Roland Casey. And you're Mrs. Humphrey, I assume? Let's find a table," he suggested and led her over to a corner with some privacy. After going to the counter for coffee for two, he sat down and got right to the matter at hand.

"My fiancée found a little dog about a week ago and she ran an ad on Craigslist as well as the local paper, and you believe that this is your dog, am I right so far?"

"Yes, that's about it. And please call me Shimmer — it's my stage name and when-ever someone says 'Mrs. Humphrey' I think my ex-mother-in-law is behind me," she said with an overdone shudder and batting of her obviously false lashes.

Roland smiled politely and went on with his questions. "Can you tell me what hap-pened with your dog?"

"Shimmer" looked uneasy and cleared her throat. "My boyfriend gave it to me for my birthday and it was a cute little thing and all, but I don't think he knew how much work it was going to be. I work long nights and I need to sleep during the day and the little thing was just all over the place. It was a destructive critter, too. I can't tell you how many pairs of fishnets it tore up and how many shoes got ruined. Those things are part of my costume and it was messing with my livelihood," she said heatedly.

Whether the dog in question was Domino or not, it was plain to see that the woman didn't like the dog, which Roland hoped would make things easier for him. "Do you have a picture of your dog? What did you name it?"

"I hadn't really settled on a name, I was still calling it Puppy-dog," she said with another shrug. "But I have some pictures on my phone. Here they are," she said, thrusting her iPhone at him.

He saw at once that the pictures were of Domino. She was smaller in the pictures but her markings were identical; it was definitely Alana's little girl. He returned the phone to the woman and repeated the question that he'd asked before, the one she hadn't answered.

"So what happened to your dog, Mrs. Humphrey?"

She batted her mascara-crusted lashes again and smiled archly.

"You were going to call me Shimmer, remember? Well, it was tearing up so much stuff and keeping me awake barking and carrying on that I had to start tying it out in the yard and one day it just wasn't there," she said opening her hands wide. "I guess the rope broke or something, but it was gone."

"Did you put up flyers or anything, run an ad for her return?" Roland asked in a carefully neutral voice.

"I meant to, but I just didn't have time. Like I said, I work nights and I sleep days. But I saw your fiancée's ad and I thought I should call to see if it was my dog in the ad. What do you think?"

Roland didn't answer in haste; he drank his now-lukewarm coffee and gave the woman a mirthless smile.

"If this is your dog, do you want it returned to you?" He didn't have to wait for an answer, because she blurted it out immediately.

"No way," she said fervently. "I broke up with the man who gave it to me and I really don't have room in my life for a dog, so no, I don't. Y'all can keep it if you want to. I just thought I should at least check and see if it was mine."

Roland reached inside his leather jacket

and retrieved the papers Royce had prepared for him. It was a bill of sale transferring ownership of Domino from Mrs. Humphrey to Roland and Alana. It was written in plain English, but so cleverly phrased that it would be impossible for "Shimmer" to change her mind about the sale.

He very smoothly explained to her what it was and then he turned on the charm.

"I just want to have some paperwork on hand to make it easy to prove that Alana has the dog with your permission. Also, because I know how expensive it is to own a dog, I want to compensate you for all the money you spent on vet bills, food, grooming and training," he said, giving her an easy smile that made her push her frightening boobs out even further.

She quickly signed the contract while he counted out five hundred dollars in crisp one-hundred-dollar bills.

"Shimmer, I really appreciate you taking the time to try and locate your dog, and I thank you for meeting with me so we could get this handled. You're a very kind and classy lady."

Shimmer was thrilled with the unexpected cash and she practically flew out of Starbucks, no doubt about to embark on a spending spree. Or maybe she was just going to replace her shoes and fishnets, Roland didn't care. He just wanted to make sure that nobody could ever take Domino away from Alana. Losing her beloved pup would break her heart and that was never going to happen as long as he had the power to prevent it. He'd planned on giving Shimmer Humphrey one thousand dollars, but when he realized how little she cared for Domino he cut the amount in half.

He grinned as he headed back to his truck because he'd decided to get something nice for Alana. He couldn't wait to see her smile when she opened the box.

He just couldn't wait to see her, period.

CHAPTER 9

"So, tell me exactly how your hair came to be in this condition," Alexis asked archly.

Alana was in Alexis's private work area at her lead spa, Sanctuary One. She had decided to work a half day at Custom Classics and called Alexis to see if she felt like rescuing her mane and the result was a skillful interrogation by Alexis while Ava babysat Domino. She sighed in resignation while Alexis combed out the tangled mass of hair.

"Why do I have the feeling that you already know more than you should?" she answered. She closed her eyes, both to avoid seeing Alexis's satisfied smirk and because her sister's fingers were like magic, sending relaxing sensations down her scalp and through her body. No wonder most of Alexis's clients fell asleep in the chair.

"It's because I do know most of your business, Alana. I know you way too well and I know that something momentous and fabulous happened to you. If you'd come in here with your hair looking perfect instead of looking like a dollar-store Afro wig, I'd still know that something has changed. I can feel it," she said emphatically. "Besides, I had a dream about it."

"You did not," Alana contradicted her.

"Yes, I did. I've been dreaming a lot lately and I dreamed that you were getting married. To Roland, as a matter of fact. It was so serene and beautiful and you were so happy. If I didn't already know that he was in love with you, I would have blown it off, but since I had some insider information, it made perfect sense."

Alana could feel her cheeks get hot but she also felt her heart rate increase. "What are you babbling about? What inside information?"

This time Alexis looked a little embarrassed. "I think this is one of the side benefits of impending motherhood. I'm having all these dreams, I can't keep my hands off my husband and I also can't keep my mouth shut. I shouldn't have said anything to you, I should have pretended like I didn't know about his feelings. Blame it on the baby," she said dramatically.

"Girl, if you don't quit being a drama queen I'm going to scream. You have thirty seconds to tell me why you said Roland is in love with me. Twice," she added, holding up two fingers.

"Okay, okay, I'll tell you," Alexis said, leading her over to the shampoo bowl.

Alana sat down while Alexis adjusted her headrest. While she reached for the shampoo, Alexis said, "Jared told me that Roland was crazy about you. He said that Roland was like a VanBuren when it came to finding a soul mate — he said as soon as he set eyes on you that he knew you were the one."

"When did he tell you this? And why didn't you tell me before?"

"He told me at Sherri's reception. And I didn't tell you because if you'd known even for a minute that the man had feelings for you, you would've run like a thief in the night. So I kept my big mouth shut and let nature take its course. And it did, which is why you came in here looking like an electrified porcupine. It was worth it, wasn't it?"

Alana's stern expression melted away into a beautiful smile. "It was absolutely worth it. Lexie, I can't believe I'm saying this, but I'm so happy that I met Roland. I'm happy he didn't turn and run when I wouldn't give him the time of day and I'm really happy that his car got wrecked."

"You're what? He was in an accident and Jared didn't tell me?"

Alana could hear the genuine concern in her sister's voice and hastened to explain about the '67 T-bird. "If he hadn't brought the car all the way from Chicago for Custom Classics to work on, we wouldn't have started talking. Once we really started talking and getting to know each other, everything just fell into place. I already liked him of course — I thought he was a really sweet guy. I felt comfortable with him and I was able to just concentrate on him and let the past stay in the past," she told her.

"How does Domino like him? She's extremely gorgeous, by the way. You have to bring her over for a playdate with Sookie and Honeybee. They're very good with other dogs, she'll have a ball," Alexis said as she applied conditioner to Alana's hair.

"I'm taking her over to Mama's house tomorrow so she can meet Sparkle. And so Mama can grill me. I'm sure her antenna is up by now. You know how she is, no secret is safe with her," Alana said with a laugh. She didn't say anything else after that; her eyes grew distant and she bit the corner of her lower lip, something that indicated when she was deep in thought. Alexis picked up on it right away.

"What's on your mind, Lana? You have that overthinking look on your face."

"I'm not overthinking, I'm just wondering, why me? How do I get to be so lucky? What if I'd never met Roland and what if I mess it up?"

"Sweetie, that's what we call overthinking. When you start the who-what-when-where thing, that means you're trying to overanalyze something. Just enjoy it, Alana, and stop trying to dissect every aspect of it. Suppose I hadn't gotten a flat tire, does that mean I would have never met Jared? I doubt it. We would have found each other sooner or later because it was meant to be. Just like you and Roland."

Before Alana could respond, Ava walked into the private salon with Domino, who gave a yip of joy at seeing Alana.

"She's so cute, can I have her?" asked Ava.

"Nope, she's all mine, aren't you, little girl?" Ava deposited her on Alana's lap and Domino licked her hand happily.

"So what's up with you and Roland? When did all this happen?" Ava asked as she checked her appearance in the mirror.

Alana frowned at Alexis, who frowned at Ava, who looked innocent. "Have you been listening at doors again?" Alexis said with exasperation in her voice.

"No, but I'm not blind, either," Ava answered. "Besides, he had this delivered to you," she added, belatedly handing a heavy cream parchment envelope over to Alana.

Alana held it in one hand and ran her fingers over its smooth surface before opening it. It was a beautiful card inviting her and Domino to dinner at his loft at 8:00 p.m. Ava was reading over her shoulder and her eyes widened.

" 'A car will be there to collect you at seven-thirty,' " she recited. "Dang, you women have all the luck. I never meet anybody like that," she said with a little pout.

"Maybe if you move out of Mama's house you might have a chance," Alexis said kindly.

Alana didn't say anything because her thoughts were racing. There was only one thing on her mind at the moment, the question that consumes every woman when she's offered the evening of her dreams with a wonderful man. She looked at Alexis and waved the card, asking plaintively, "What am I going to wear?"

Alana's eyes were shining with happiness in the glow of the candlelight. It had been a perfect evening in every sense of the word. With Alexis's help, not to mention her photographic memory of Alana's closet, she'd come up with the perfect outfit to wear. It was an off-the-shoulder cashmere sweater in a beautiful shade of soft aqua. Alexis had given it to her for Christmas and she hadn't worn it yet.

Happy that she'd saved it for such an occasion, she paired it with slim-fitting pants that fit like leggings. They were a rich cream color with a gold sheen, a gift from Adrienne that had also not seen the light of day until now. Alana was the first to admit that her social life was lacking, but she had a feeling that it was going to be a lot more active now. Her hair and makeup were perfect and she smelled heavenly, thanks to a tester she'd gotten when she'd ordered some perfume for her mother. It smelled better than anything she'd ever worn, which improved her already happy mood.

She thought that Roland was going to call for her, but when she opened the door there was a real limousine with a driver, with whom Domino flirted, as usual. On the ride to the loft, she tried to imagine what Roland had in mind for the date, but she gave up because she knew whatever it was would be wonderful and she was right.

When she and Domino arrived at the loft, it was like something out of a movie. He greeted them at the door, kissing her on both cheeks and picking up Domino, who was dancing around in circles at the end of her leash. He was dressed in a sexy, sophisticated manner, but very casual at the same time. He had on a V-necked sweater in navy and a pair of really nice jeans.

"You look beautiful," he told her, standing back to take a look at her from head to toe. "Your hair looks gorgeous and I promise not to get it wet tonight."

"You look very handsome," she returned. "What's the occasion, Roland?"

"We're celebrating," he said as he bent to put Domino on the floor and unhook her leash.

"What are we celebrating?"

"Us."

And it was a celebration in every way. Roland had candles everywhere, although they were all well out of Domino's reach. Music was playing, the dining room table was set for two and there were white tulips on the big coffee table and a fire in the glass-enclosed gas fireplace.

It was extremely romantic and she told him so as he showed her around the loft. It was furnished for comfort and fashion, with a huge sectional sofa in a navy material that was incredibly soft and cushiony. There was a giant flat-screen on the wall and several beautiful plants that gave the place a homey air despite its size. Alana was touched to see that he also had a soft, comfortable-looking doggie bed with several toys for Domino near the sofa.

The meal he served was superb and featured some of her favorite things like salmon, scallops, rice pilaf and the best white wine she'd ever had.

Domino had her own dinner from an over-the-top dining set that consisted of a set of ceramic dishes in a wrought-iron stand; Alana recognized it as a designer creation that she'd seen in a magazine. Even though the ambiance was formal and well-planned, the atmosphere was relaxed and the conversation was easy. It was easily the nicest date she'd ever had.

"I feel like I'm in a movie," she told him. "Like the heroine in one of those Audrey Hepburn movies with handsome Cary Grant as the hero."

"Seriously? So who'd be playing your part?"

"Barbara McNair," she said at once. "Nobody seems to talk about her anymore, but she was this beautiful black singer/actress. She was so talented. And you'd be played by somebody like Harry Belafonte.

Can you sing? If you can, it could be a musical."

"You have quite the imagination. If you're finished we can have dessert now or later, your choice."

She opted for later and he made her go to the living room to relax while he made quick work of the dishes. Domino was in heaven in the big open space; she was racing around like a tiny filly on a racetrack. When Roland joined her on the giant sofa, he was amazed at the way she was running around.

"Papillons have a lot of energy for their size, which is why they need a lot of exercise. I think I should get her a playmate so they can bounce off each other," Alana said, sliding closer to Roland.

He pulled her onto his lap and buried his face in the crook of her neck. "Damn, you smell good. What are you wearing?"

Alana made a soft purring sound before answering. His goatee felt so good against her neck that she had to force herself to concentrate. "Mmm, it's called Mademoiselle Piguet. I only have a sample of it, but I think I'm going to have to treat myself to a whole bottle."

"You should wear that all the time," he said. "It smells just like you."

Further words were unnecessary for a while because the long luscious kisses they exchanged communicated their feelings much better. His hands were around her waist and slid up to her breasts and she moved to give him better access. He was just about to slide into home base when Domino decided that she wasn't getting enough attention and she executed a mighty leap onto Alana's lap.

"Yeah, we're definitely getting you a partner in crime, baby girl," Roland muttered. "How about I take you out and then put you to bed so I can be alone with my lady? How does that sound?" It sounded fine, as Domino dashed off to get her leash.

"You don't have to keep her out too long," Alana said helpfully. "I can take her out for a good run in the backyard when we go home."

Roland put both his arms around her and held her tight while he gave her a searing-hot kiss. "You're not going anywhere, honey. You're spending the night," he said with a very confident smile.

"But I don't have any clothes or anything," she pointed out. "Unlike you, I don't keep a change in my car, which I don't have anyway."

"Leave it all to me, Alana. I got this," he

told her as he put on his jacket. Domino was eager to go so there was no time for more discussion.

She watched the two of them leave and sank down into the heavenly soft cushions of the sofa, thinking about Roland and how happy he made her. Everything about him was lovable, sexy and strong.

She was so comfortable that her eyes closed and when Roland came back, she was curled up with her arms around a pillow, sound asleep. He coaxed Domino onto her new bed with the aid of a couple of her homemade cookies and she settled down happily.

Roland went around the large space blowing out candles and watching Alana sleep before picking her up and carrying her into the bedroom. She stirred slightly, but she didn't wake up until she was in the middle of his king-size bed.

"Did I miss something? How did we get in here?"

Roland grinned at her from his standing position. "You don't remember me dragging you in here by your hair?"

Alana's face broke into a big smile. "That I would have remembered." She wiggled her toes and asked where her shoes were. "I don't want a repeat of past behavior. No matter what I give her to chew on, Domino seems to like my shoes the best, bless her little heart."

"I put them out of harm's way. By the way, you were saying something about not having anything for tomorrow," Roland said as he opened the antique armoire. Hanging on the door was a new set of underwear in a pale peach color, plus a pair of jeans and a beautiful coral sweater. "There's even a new toothbrush just for you. I told you I had it handled."

Alana was so touched that tears came to her eyes. She rose to a kneeling position as he came to join her on the bed. She locked her arms around his neck and kissed him thoroughly. "You are, without a doubt, the sweetest, most thoughtful man in the world. Thank you so much for doing this for me. And for all you've done for Domino. She loves her new toys almost as much as she loves you."

Roland returned the kiss with interest and this time there was no interruption as he slipped his hand under her sweater and slid it deftly over her head. His sweater followed it, and then her pants came off. He was about to remove his jeans but he paused to go to his dresser and retrieve something. He sat behind Alana on the bed so that she was between his legs and he held the object up so she could see it.

It was the most astounding necklace she'd ever seen. On a thin rose-gold chain dangled a beautiful teardrop that had four bands of tiny stones intersecting at the top and bottom. The teardrop was a soft rose quartz and the tiny diamonds were cinnamon and chocolate-colored. Alana gasped in surprise.

"Do you like it?"

"I love it," she said softly. She touched it with one finger and sighed. "It's so amazing, Roland. How can I ever thank you?"

"You don't have to thank me. You just have to enjoy it, honey." He fastened the clasp and she turned around to show him how it looked. He was so busy looking at the expression on her face that he didn't pay much attention to the necklace, other than noticing how pretty the rose gold looked against her skin.

She picked up the teardrop with her fingers and looked down at it before leaning forward to kiss him again. Unfastening the front of her champagne-colored strapless bra, she tossed it onto the bed and said, "One of us is overdressed. What are you going to do about that?"

In about ten seconds, he showed her.

"Come here, gorgeous," Roland said in a low, sexy growl.

He was now magnificently bare and ready for her. Alana had one knee on the edge of the bed and one hand on one of the thick posts of the four-poster bed. She looked both sexy and innocent, wearing only her thong and the necklace. She held out her free hand and he took it, pulling her on top of him. The contact with his warm skin made her melt against him.

"Mmm, baby, you feel so good," she whispered. "You're so warm. Why are you so warm? Are you a werewolf or something?"

His deep laugh made his pecs move in a way that made her sensitized nipples bloom even more. Her hips began to move as she sought to get even closer to him.

"I'm not a lycan, sweetheart, but I'm pretty sure that you're some kind of witch because you drive me crazy. I'm hot because you make me that way. I'm going to have to start wearing a cup all day because I think about you and my pal jumps to attention. And I think about you all day, so that's a problem."

She acknowledged the compliment with a giggle and confessed that she had the same issue. "Miss Alana can't seem to behave herself when you're on my mind."

He turned so that she was on the bottom and began to lick his way down her neck, stopping when he reached the critical spot between her breasts. Suddenly he stopped, which made her gasp in frustration.

"Who is Miss Alana?"

By way of answer she took his hand and placed it on the moist spot between her legs. "Meet Miss Alana. She likes you a lot and she's getting impatient."

Roland tried to hold in his laughter, but failed miserably. "That's another reason I love you. I've never met a woman who could make me laugh and arouse me at the same time. And I really don't want to keep Miss Alana waiting," he said before going back to the task at hand.

He tongued the space between her breasts while sliding his hand into her thong and exploring the moist treasure that awaited him. When he moved his mouth to her nipple, he began to manipulate her nub, stroking it over and over while licking and sucking her in the same rhythm until he could feel her begin to throb. When the movement of her hips grew more fevered and she was moaning and sighing and saying his name, he relented slightly and changed positions. He kissed his way down to her navel, lingering there while he removed her thong at last, burying his face between her legs.

Her first orgasm came within seconds; he'd barely begun to taste her sweetness when he felt her juices begin to flow and her tight muscles contract. Her back arched and he put his hands under her smooth rounded bottom so that he could hold her against his mouth; he wasn't finished yet. The more she trembled and cried out, the more he tasted and tongued her, drinking in everything she offered.

He used his tongue to explore her over and over until she came apart in his hands two more times. He finally joined their bodies in one swift motion while she wrapped her legs around his waist and her arms went around his neck. Their bodies moved as one, pumping and thrusting as he rose to his knees so he could penetrate her even more deeply. The friction increased until a mutual climax rocked them into the most intense sensation Roland had ever experienced.

They collapsed onto the bed in a sweaty, trembling tangle, their bodies heaving as the tremors gradually slowed down.

Alana's head was cradled on Roland's shoulder and he held her as though she was his entire world, tenderly and tightly. He kissed her sweet-smelling hair as they lay entwined, bathed in the soft glow of the lamp.

Sleep seemed to be the next step but neither one of them was ready to let go of the moment. Alana's hand stroked his chest in slow circles, palming his still-hard nipple and sending waves of sensation through his body. He caught her fingers in his hand and kissed them.

"We're using protection from now on, sweetheart. If it's not too late," he murmured.

"What does that mean?" Her voice sounded sexy, sleepy and satisfied.

"I think we might have just made a baby, Alana. I never felt anything like that before. I've always heard that when you love someone you know when it happens."

Alana's body went still and he could hear an odd distance grow when she spoke. "I don't think so, Roland. I don't think I can have a child. Ever."

Chapter 10

Most men would have been happy to hear that they'd dodged the bullet of fatherhood, but Roland wasn't most men. He was a man who was completely in love for the first time in his adult life and anything that affected the woman he loved affected him deeply.

He was calm and supportive as Alana explained that the bullet that had ended her baby's brief life had left scarring that could prevent her from carrying another child. Her recitation of the facts was short and to the point with almost no emotion in her voice. They were still naked in the bed as she told him; he was propped up on the big down pillows and she was still in his arms.

"And that's that," she ended simply. "I haven't been back to the gynecologist for any testing because it didn't matter to me. I knew that after I lost Sam and our baby that I was done with all of it. I was never going to be involved with another man and it just wasn't important. I was through with love, with marriage, with men, everything," she said, raising one small hand and dropping it lifelessly. She moved so that she was looking directly at him.

"But then my beautiful sister met a wonderful man named Jared. And Jared fell in love with her and introduced her to his loving family and his best friend. So I got to meet his best friend who is handsome and caring and sexy and sweet. He's very patient, too, because I wasn't interested in him or any other man," she said in a soft, loving tone. "I was completely wrong about that, the way I've been wrong about a lot of things in my life. And he jumped over the wall I'd hidden behind for so long and he rescued me. I fell madly in love with him and he makes me feel like the most amazing woman in the world. I would give anything to make him as happy as he makes me, but I don't know if a baby is a part of the package. I just don't know," she sighed.

Roland studied her face, loving every feature and desiring her even more than before. When she finished talking he tipped her chin up so that he could kiss her. It wasn't a long kiss, but it was powerful — sweet and binding. "We'll deal with it when we need to. In the meantime, what comes first, more lovemaking, dessert or a hot bath?"

Her eyes sparkled and she said, "Dessert!" with a teasing smile.

"Whatever your heart desires, my love," he said.

After he put on a robe and went to get dessert, Alana got out of the bed and tidied it up, thinking all the while that she was a very, very lucky woman.

Even after the intense conversation they'd had, the next few weeks seemed to fly by for both Alana and Roland. They fell into a routine that was extremely pleasant; evenings spent in just being together, a housewarming party at Adrienne's and a birthday party for Lucas.

Today was no exception; the women were meeting at Alexis's house for their annual clothing and cosmetic swap while the guys were at the loft watching ESPN until it was time to head to work. They were also dog-sitting since the sight of so many shoes and pretty clothes might prove too tempting for the doggies, especially Domino, who was still having a love affair with anything that sparkled.

So the loft was filled with Sherri and Lucas's Westies, Jared and Alexis's corgis and Domino and they were all having a ball running around on the hardwood floors, chasing each other when they weren't going from lap to lap getting their ears scratched and sneaking smooches.

At the moment, Domino was happily enjoying Royce's company, flirting for all she was worth. Jared and Roland were in the kitchen having a long talk while Lucas entertained the corgis.

The Westies were chasing each other from one end of the loft to the other and playing a masterful game of hide-and-seek. Royce raised an eyebrow at Lucas.

"I've never been around men who like being married as much as you and your brother," he said frankly.

Lucas grinned at him. "I know, a lot of people think the men in my family are kinda weird that way, but it works for us."

Royce wiped one of Domino's more passionate kisses away while assuring Lucas that he meant just the opposite. "No, man, I was paying you a compliment," he assured him. "I envy the two of you. From the looks of things, Roland is going to be the next to take the vows and he's gonna be walking around with that twenty-four-hour Colgate smile just like you VanBurens. I'ma be honest with you — I've reached a point in my life where I want what you have. I'm tired of dating, I'm tired of relationships and I want a family of my own."

Lucas looked impressed with his friend's honesty. "Half the battle — no, three-quarters of the battle is knowing what you want. Now you just have to get after it. Alana still has two single sisters, you know. And they're both fine. Beauty runs deep in that family, man, as well as brains and personality. You really couldn't ask for more," he said with the smile of a man who already has more than his share of love and happiness.

Royce nodded his head thoughtfully and said, "Odd that you should mention those ladies, Lucas. I have a definite interest in one of the Sharp sisters, as a matter of fact. I've been using my workload as an excuse, but it's time to get a move on."

Lucas raised his glass of iced tea high in a brotherly salute. "Get on it. As my daughter told me when she asked me to marry her mother, 'No pain, no gain, no gain, no glory.' Go for it, and may the force be with you, dude."

Their laughter could be heard in the kitchen where Jared and Roland were deep in conversation. Jared rubbed his unshaven cheek and grinned at his oldest and closest friend. He could tell from the way Roland kept glancing at the clock and fiddling with his cell phone that something was on his mind.

"You've got it real bad, man. You're as bad as I was before I put a ring on it. You're counting the minutes until you see your baby. Don't deny it," he warned him in a teasing voice.

Roland frowned at his friend. "I'm not trying to deny anything, Jared. Yeah, I got it bad and yeah, I'm thinking about Alana. You've been through it. You know what it's like to wake up without her next to you, especially when you have one of those red-hot dreams about her. You start to feel like some kind of perverted stalker because you're thinking about her 24/7, wondering where she is, what she's doing, how she's feeling. Whoever said that men run the world is a damned liar because you and I both know that women are the ones in control," he said glumly.

"And before you get on my case, remember that I'm the one who had to drive down here with you and two wild puppies so you could be here for her birthday and every word out of your mouth was Alexis this and Alexis that. You were so far gone that if she hadn't said 'yes' we would've had to have you committed, and you know this," he said with an evil grin.

"I'd like to say that you're presenting a revisionist history, but the truth is the light," Jared said with a bright red highlighting his cheekbones. "But that's all behind me now. We got married, got a beautiful house, two beautiful dogs, and in a few weeks we'll have the first of many children. I have an amazing, sexy, brilliant and gorgeous wife and I've never been happier in my life. So when are you going to follow in my footsteps? What are you waiting for?"

"I'm having the ring made, for your information, and I plan to give it to her on her birthday along with the keys to our new house. The house is slowing me down because I haven't found the right place. I haven't actually talked to her about another place yet because her house is really nice," he said, getting up from the stool at the work island and going to the refrigerator.

Jared looked thoughtful. "Yeah, I see what you mean. It's a great little bungalow and she's made it look like something out of a magazine, but once you start having kids, it's going to feel like a shoebox."

"Alana is a magician, isn't she? The way the T-bird turned out is amazing," he said with a grin. "The insurance company wrote it off and she and her crew made it look like it had just rolled off the line. She did the paint job herself," he said proudly. "She's truly good at what she does, but I'll be happy when she starts painting full-time and starts fulfilling her own dreams." He paused and looked uncomfortable before continuing.

"This is just between the two of us," he said solemnly. "Alana is convinced that she can't have children."

Jared looked stunned as Roland tersely repeated what Alana had told him. "Afterward, she just blocked it out in a way. She said she never intended to get involved with another man as long as she lived so it didn't matter. And to tell you the truth, it doesn't matter to me, not one bit. If she can't have children we can adopt, or borrow our nieces and nephews or just get a bunch of dogs," he said as the Westies careened around the work island on their way to another adventure.

"All I want is Alana. I'm taking her to Chicago to meet the folks again so she'll understand that she'll be marrying into a really strange family," he laughed. "My mother thinks she'll be a wonderful wife for me and she can't wait to see her again. I just hope my sisters don't make her crazy."

"Alana is used to crazy sisters, Ro. She's got three of her own," Jared pointed out.

"True dat. You wanna help me make sandwiches for those louts in the living room or should we order subs?"

"Are you kidding? Order food for them and make them pay for ours," Jared said and they bumped fists in agreement.

"Can I have this sweater?" Ava pleaded, plucking at the sleeve of the fabulous coral sweater.

"No, Ava, you can't. We're swapping things that we don't wear or don't care for or can't wear. I have the sweater on, which means I do wear it. Besides, it was a gift from Roland, so forget about it," Alana said.

Once a year the sisters and Sherri got together after clearing their closets of clothes that were no longer in first rotation. The idea was to give their siblings first dibs on the items before they went to charity.

It was a good deal all around because they all wore the same size and, with the exception of Adrienne, had the same basic taste in clothes. There were often items that had only been worn once and in some cases, still had the price tags on them. The same went for cosmetics. A fragrance that had fallen out of favor, an excess of body wash or lotion, there were many good things to be exchanged. Besides that, it provided the women a chance to get together and talk for hours.

Alexis wasn't terribly interested in clothes; she was focused on the impending birth of her first child. She was stretched out on the chaise end of the sofa in the solarium, offering suggestions, but that was the limit of her participation. Sherri was stretched out on the other end of the sofa napping. She was in the early weeks of her pregnancy, but all she wanted to do was sleep. Sydney was having a playdate and since Lucas was, too, she was taking full advantage.

Adrienne, who wasn't nearly as far along in her pregnancy as Alexis, but past the sleepytime stage, was trying to talk her mother into trying on a dress, one of her original creations. It was a striking combination of bright yellow silk matched to two different prints and Adrienne assured her that it would look fabulous on her. Aretha wasn't too sure.

"Don't you think it's too young for me? I think my days of wearing bright colors like that are over," she said with a wistful sigh.

Alana took the dress from Adrienne and insisted that her mother try it on. "Come with me, Mama. I think Adrienne is right. I can see you in this little number."

They went into the guest room and Aretha grudgingly took off her clothes and slipped into the dress. It was fascinating to watch the transition on her mother's face as Alana showed her how to fasten the wrap dress properly. It was a perfect fit for her still-slender figure and instead of looking loud or gaudy, it looked timeless and utterly chic. The elbow-length sleeves and deep V-neck were designed to complement any woman's figure. The skirt flared out with godets inset all the way around, which gave the fluttery fabric a better hang. The medley of prints was perfect as all three fabrics were combined in an obi sash that made her small waist look tiny. Aretha was thrilled.

"I told you, Mama, you make the dress yours. You're wearing the dress instead of the other way around."

They talked about possible accessories and Alana got a real kick out of seeing how the dress lifted her mother's spirits. Aretha turned to her with a smile.

"Thank you for taking the time to show me the error of my fashion ways," she said. "I'm going to love wearing this dress. My girls certainly are a talented group."

"Yes, we are. How do you like the portrait I did of Adrienne? You saw it at her house, didn't you?"

"I did and it's wonderful. I wish you were dedicating your life to your painting, Alana. That's your true gift. You can sell the shop, or hire someone to run it for you. You should be painting all the time, not just when you can fit it in," Aretha said firmly, but not in a bossy or demanding way.

"Have you been talking to Roland? Because that sounds exactly like him," Alana said with a wry smile. "Are you two ganging up on me?"

"Will it work? Because if it will, I'll be more than happy to. I knew I liked that young man for something other than his good looks and good manners — he's got a good head on his shoulders and he is completely dedicated to you, Alana. That's a man who wants nothing but your happiness and he'll do everything in the world to make sure you have all your heart desires. Trust me, honey. A mother knows these things," she said smugly.

"Mama, you never cease to amaze me," Alana said fondly. "I was truly surprised at how quickly you took to Roland. I was afraid you were going to warn me against him and tell me how wrong he was for me and all of that stuff," she admitted.

Aretha sat down on the bed next to her

eldest daughter and took both of her hands. Squeezing them gently, she said, "Sweetheart, unless he was a sociopath or a fortune hunter or something, I wouldn't have said anything of the kind. I'm happy for you, Alana, I'm happy for you both. After you lost Sam and the baby I was so frightened for you. You don't remember much of those first weeks after he was killed, but I remember every second of every minute of that terrible time. You were so consumed with grief after the tragedy that I was afraid I was going to lose you, too.

"When you recovered and you were able to handle things again, you'd closed yourself off from anything resembling a man but that actually didn't worry me as much because I knew in my heart that when you met the right person you'd come around. I never told you this because daughters have a habit of doing the opposite of what their mothers say," she said with a warm smile, "but the first time I saw the way Roland looked at you I wanted to do a happy dance because I knew that he was the one. And he knew it, too. It took you a little while to catch up, but you're there now and that's all that matters."

Alana was staring at her mother in amazement while Aretha went back to admiring her reflection in the mirror. "So when is the wedding? Have you talked about it?"

"No, not really. We've only been together for a couple of months, Mama. I'm sure the topic will come up at some point."

"Oh, it certainly will. Just don't let me get down the aisle before you do," Aretha said with a wink.

"Huh?"

"Your father and I are getting married again," she said cheerfully.

"Seriously? That's wonderful news, Mama. You never should have gotten divorced in the first place."

"I know but I'm a stubborn woman and your daddy can be a donkey when he wants to, so there you have it. We're probably going to have a very small ceremony and then take a cruise to Alaska to see the northern lights next January or February. It'll be nice and cold and I can wear fabulous sweaters and we can cuddle all night," she said gleefully. "I was kidding about me beating you to the altar, but I really can't wait to see the two of you happily married."

Alana gave her a salute. "I'll do my best, General."

Aretha continued to preen in the mirror, turning to look over her shoulder. "I'm more of a queen, don't you think?"

"Absolutely, Your Majesty, I hear and obey. Come show Adrienne how the dress looks," she urged.

"You know, I'm worried about Adrienne. I don't care what she says about those flighty bird-brained people being her friends, she needs legal representation. It was a huge mistake to enter into that damned surrogacy with those idiots and no matter how much they claim to not want the baby, she needs the counsel of a good lawyer. I'm going to ask Royce Griffin to have a talk with her."

"Sounds like a good idea, Mama."

"Of course it is. Mama knows best," she said airily as she sashayed back to the solarium.

CHAPTER 11

Alana checked her reflection in the mirror one more time. After the swap meet at Alexis's house, she'd come home loaded with swag and decided to take a long bubble bath to get ready for her evening with Roland.

Now she was moisturized, creamed, lotioned and perfumed and ready for an evening of intimacy. She had a surprise for him, too, in the form of another of Adrienne's creations. It was undoubtedly the sexiest thing she'd ever worn and she loved the fact that her sister had made it.

The fabric was silk, hand-dyed by Adrienne in a fantastic ombre range of pink from the palest to a deep rose. The bodice was halter-necked and slightly bloused before crossing over into the waistband. The skirt was cut on the bias and opened on the side with a leg-revealing thigh-high split. It flared out to the ankle and it was so soft and sexy that she decided to go bare underneath it all. The back was so low-cut she couldn't have worn a bra anyway, so she went for it.

She wore her hair up in a twist adorned with some pretty pink chopsticks she'd gotten from Adrienne as a trade for a leather tote bag. Her only jewelry was her rose gold necklace from Roland, along with the matching earrings he'd also given her. She even polished her fingernails, something she did very rarely.

As a last touch, she used the bottle of Mademoiselle Piguet, another gift from Roland. He spoiled her something awful and she loved it. He was the most generous man she'd ever known. Sam had been a caring and giving man, but he hadn't had the same kind of inclinations that Roland possessed. He even doted on Domino, treating her like she was a family member and not just a pet.

Roland was just . . . everything. And tonight was her chance to dote on him for a change.

She didn't get a chance to cook for him very often because he always took over the kitchen chores. Sometimes they went out to Seven-Seventeen, or he took her to someplace else with fabulous food and great music.

But tonight, she'd fixed him a meal that she was sure he'd enjoy. He liked good food, not fancy food. Nouvelle cuisine and micro gastronomy and other fads were of no interest to him. He preferred homestyle food, as long as it was properly prepared. She was no gourmet cook, but she was good with the basics. Aretha had made sure that her girls would be able to take care of themselves when they left the nest and that included being able to cook.

Braised short ribs, macaroni and cheese and greens were on the menu tonight, along with homemade yeast rolls and a chocolate cake for dessert. Everything had been made before she'd left for the swap meet and all she had to do was warm it up, toss a salad and make the salad dressing. She was about to begin the dressing when two brief rings of the bell signaled that Roland was home with Domino.

She hurried to the door and tried to look seductive as she opened it. Judging by the look on his face, she succeeded.

While Domino did her happy dance of love around Alana's feet, Roland stared at her with deep admiration. She picked up Domino, who wriggled happily in her arms while he walked around her in total awe.

"You look . . . incredible, Alana," he said

slowly. "You look fantastic. And I hate to do this to you because you've obviously gone to a lot of trouble, but I hope whatever smells so good can be heated up because dinner is going to be late."

He took Domino from her and placed her on the floor. "Bedtime, sweetie. Go to bed."

Alana's eyes widened as he reached for her and pulled her into a passionate kiss before picking her up and carrying her to the bedroom while still making love to her mouth every step of the way.

The kiss ended as he deposited her on the bed and the soft silk of the dress parted to reveal her equally silky legs. He was smiling and unbuttoning his shirt at the same time, not saying a word.

"Aren't you hungry?" Laughter colored her voice as she asked the question.

"Starving," he answered.

"Don't you want to eat?"

"I plan to," he said, tossing his shirt over his shoulder. His body looked magnificent in the soft light of the lamp on the dresser. With every step he took towards her, she felt a pulse of anticipation ripple through her body.

Alana scooted up to the head of the bed and watched with great anticipation as Roland kicked off his loafers before removing his jeans. He looked wild and ravenous as he mounted the bed like a jungle cat stalking his prey. She crossed her arms to unhook the straps behind her neck but he was too quick for her. His hands grasped her ankles and pulled her towards him until she was on her back with her knees bent slightly. Roland took one of her feet and kissed it, running his tongue along the instep. A breathy laugh escaped her and she rose up on her elbows to stare at her lover.

"What are you doing?"

"I love your feet. They're so sexy, just like the rest of you."

Profoundly glad she'd also polished her toenails, Alana gasped as he sucked her toes gently before turning his attention to her long legs. He rubbed his face against her calf while stroking her thigh, licking his way up to the tender treasure that awaited him.

Sliding his hands up to her hips, he was both surprised and delighted to find that his lady was going commando under the dreamy dress. He turned his full attention to her at once, aiming to satisfy her hunger completely. It was a part of making love to Alana that he loved, paying homage to her with the most intimate kiss possible.

His tongue explored her, adored her and brought her the ultimate pleasure so quickly that he couldn't stop until he felt the throbbing of her jewel begin again. Her hips were twisting wildly and the sounds that came from her throat were like a mating cry that he had to answer.

In seconds he was deep inside his woman, pushing and thrusting. He was so big and hard that every move stroked her clit and hit her G-spot at the same time, causing her tight inner muscles to clench and release, clench and release until his body jerked and held while the magic exploded into a bliss-filled climax shared by both of them.

He held on tight, pulling her up so that he was kneeling and she was astride him with the folds of pink fabric drifting around their hips. His fingers fumbled with the hook at the back of her neck until he unfastened it while she struggled to undo the waist and she was free from the garment and their naked bodies rubbed against each other.

He thought about stopping for a moment because he didn't want to hurt her, but she was giving as good as she got and they kept on going. The new position gave them even better friction and their mouths locked together for a wildly passionate kiss as their reward rained down on them like liquid fire.

It took every bit of Roland's considerable strength to keep holding on to her trembling, wet body until they were finally at rest. Her hair was wrecked, the dress was a casualty of love and they were covered with sweat, but it was the most profound act of love two people could ever have. Now he knew beyond any certainty what it meant to be complete.

Roland was getting more animated as they got closer to the exit that would lead them to his parents' house. Alana was much less so. She'd met Roland's family on several occasions and they were lovely people, but lovely was a subjective state, prone to a huge sea of change when relationships changed.

When she was just the sister-in-law of the woman who married Roland's best friend, that was one thing. Well-bred people could always behave themselves at festive events like weddings.

Now things were different. She was coming to Chicago as Roland's woman. She was sure it would be a nice weekend, and his family would be happy to see her. Roland had told her so at least a hundred times.

"Are you sure, absolutely sure, that it's okay to bring Domino? I could have left her with Sherri or Mama. She and Sparkle get along like BFFs, it would have been fine," Alana said worriedly.

Roland took his right hand off the steering wheel and wrapped it around her neck. "You really need to chill, baby, I keep telling you that everything is going to be fine. We're going to be staying at my condo so Domino won't be underfoot. As a matter of fact, we may have trouble prying her away from my sisters. I've never seen you so jumpy and I promise you there's no reason for it. You've met my family before and they haven't changed. They're really excited about your visit."

Alana smiled wanly, but Roland couldn't see her ambivalent expression in the dark. She glanced over her shoulder and saw that Domino was still asleep in her doggie car seat. She'd proved to be an excellent traveler so far and there was no reason to think the worst, but she was uncharacteristically worried.

She didn't say anything else as they drove through a very nice residential area full of large brick houses with lawns that were undoubtedly well-kept, or would be when the weather got warmer.

It was much chillier in Chicago than in South Carolina, but Alana had dressed for the occasion. She wore a beautiful three-piece cashmere jogging set that she'd scored from her mother at the swap meet. Aretha had gotten it for an indecently low price when Neiman Marcus had its after-after Christmas sale and she'd worn it once.

"I have no idea why I thought that a cashmere outfit was a good idea for me — I'm the poster child for hot flashes these days. But I might want to borrow it for the Alaskan cruise," she'd warned as she'd swapped it for a Coach bag that Alana never used.

Roland turned into a long driveway with no warning and Alana felt her heart leap into her throat. Domino woke up when the soothing movement of the car stopped, and yawned widely before giving a little bark to let them know that it was time for a bathroom break.

"We're here," Roland said unnecessarily. He slid out of the SUV with his usual masculine grace and opened the back door of the car, putting Domino's leash on before lifting her out of the car seat.

He walked her around to Alana's side and while she was taking a dainty pee, he opened the door and held out his free hand so Alana could get out of the vehicle. Hoping that he couldn't feel her hand shaking through her leather glove, Alana finally put her feet on the cold concrete of his parents' driveway. She was at a loss for words, which was just as well because the multi-paned glass door of the big house opened and his family came out on the porch to greet them.

The next few minutes were like an ambush of affection as his sisters surrounded the couple with hugs and kisses and squeals of adoration for Domino. The next thing she knew, they were in the house and his father was taking her coat while his mother complimented her ensemble.

"Come on in, please come in and get warm. I know it's much warmer in Columbia, so let's get you a nice cup of coffee or cocoa," she said with a big smile. "You look so lovely, dear," she added, cupping Alana's face and giving her a big kiss on the cheek.

Glendora was so pretty and sweet it was easy to see that her welcome was genuine, which made Alana feel much more relaxed. Her husband, Renard, came into the living room to join them and again, the warmth and affection that radiated from him was plain to see. They sat down on the sofa together with Alana in the middle. Pamela was still cooing over Domino as she carried her into the room.

"Mommy, look! Have you ever seen anything so cute?" She placed Domino on the floor and she immediately preened and showed off her fluffy red turtleneck sweater and red booties. "Look at how Alana dressed her up! That is too much!" Pamela laughed.

Roland wandered over to a wing chair and tried to look nonchalant, but Alana ratted him out. "Pamela, your big brother bought that little ensemble for Domino. He ordered it from this really snazzy store called Canine Styles in New York and it cost more than one of my sweaters."

Laughter filled the room while Roland tried to defend himself. "She's not used to this weather. I couldn't have her getting a cold. And she has delicate feet, the salt here will bother them so she needs the boots," he protested.

All five of his sisters turned their large, bright eyes on him and laughed even harder. "He's just a big pushover," Pandora said. "Such a softie."

Glendora had given birth to a set of twins, Marisa and Megan, and a set of triplets, Pamela, Portia and Pandora. No fertility drugs of any kind were used, it was just a blessing. Multiple births were frequent in her family and she took it in stride, although her first husband had not. Pamela was always referred to as the baby, because she was the last one to leave the hospital after they were born.

They were a glorious bunch, tall and with

skin the same rich brown shade as Roland, with thick, well-cared-for dark brown hair. They all seemed to be down-to-earth and friendly as well as being funny because they continued to tease Roland without mercy. While Domino got acquainted with Glendora and Renard, they alternated between chatting up Alana and needling their beloved brother. He looked completely relieved when his brother, Glenn, came in the room, followed by a big dog.

"Ooh, what a beauty," Alana said. "Is he a Bernese mountain dog?" she asked, holding out a hand to the newcomer. He sniffed her fingers and gave her hand a lick.

"Yes, but this is a she. This is Lady Guinevere, but we call her Gwennie. She's a big softie as you can see."

It was true; Gwennie was touching noses with Domino while Renard removed her boots and sweater. She leaped off the sofa and after a few sniffs, the two dogs became instant BFFs and they trotted off for adventure.

It was beginning to feel like she was visiting her own family, not a group of strangers who might not like her. Glendora went to the kitchen to make Alana's hot chocolate and Portia showed her the powder room where she could freshen up. Minutes later they were all in the huge kitchen where Renard served up a big bowl of gumbo over rice with corn bread that had just come out of the oven. Roland sat next to her and it was impossible to disguise the fact that they were a couple in love.

"This is the best gumbo I've ever eaten in my life," Alana said happily. "And this chocolate is just plain sinful. Thank you so much."

Renard grinned proudly. "I grew up in New Orleans and Creole cooking is my specialty. I taught Roland everything he knows about down-home food."

Glendora agreed. "Renard is a much better cook than I am," she said with a rueful smile. "But it's hard to cook for a man who really knows his way around the kitchen."

"Amen to that," Alana said with a smile at Roland. "I feel like a rank amateur next to Roland."

"Don't listen to her, Ma. She made me a meal fit for a king a few weeks ago, braised short ribs, homemade yeast rolls, macaroni and cheese that's better than we serve in the restaurant and a made-from-scratch chocolate cake that melted on my tongue," he said, giving Alana a sizzling look. He didn't have to remind her that the meal was consumed after the best loving she'd ever had and that the chocolate cake had been consumed while they were naked in bed. Her cheeks were on fire and she had to change the subject quickly.

"Roland, could you be an angel and get something out of the car for me? I have a little gift for your folks," she said.

He did as she asked and returned with a large flat package wrapped in brown paper and securely tied with string. It was a surprise for him, too, because she'd hidden it under her garment bag. She handed it to Glendora with a shy smile. "I hope you like it."

Renard cut the string and when the wrapper came off, there was absolute silence in the room. Alana felt the cold fingers of panic tickle her spine. She'd thought it the perfect gift, but it appeared that she was wrong. It was a portrait of Roland stretched out on his sofa with Domino curled up on his chest.

She'd painted it with pastels and it captured the subjects perfectly. There was also another portrait of Roland smiling. This one was executed in colored pencil and it looked so realistic it was like looking at a photograph.

Glendora broke the silence with a voice filled with emotion. "Alana, these are the most beautiful things I've ever seen. I had no idea you were such a talented artist. That's my son, inside and out. You captured every nuance of him," she said.

After she finished with her thanks, everyone chimed in, praising Alana's obvious gift and the brilliance of her art. Roland was just as astounded as his family because he'd had no idea that she'd done the work.

"She's amazing," he said, standing behind her with his arms wrapped around her. "Wait until you see Black Beauty. It looks even better than it did before it got destroyed. Those pictures I sent you on the cell phone really don't do it justice. You have to see it in person so you can see the interior. Ma, it looks just like it did the day Granddad bought it."

His mother's eyes filled with tears as she looked at the portraits and then looked at her son with the woman he would love until he left this world. "Alana, restoring that car meant so much to Roland because it meant so much to my father, his grandfather. You're so good for him."

"You're the best thing that's ever happened to me," Roland whispered in her ear. She was smiling for all she was worth because everything was truly right in her world now.

CHAPTER 12

It was hard to say who was having the most fun in the Windy City, Roland, Alana or Domino. Domino had formed a bond with Gwennie and they were happy to spend hours playing while Roland and Alana were out visiting friends.

They had to go see Emily and Todd Wainwright and their growing boys, and then they had to visit with Emily's sister, Ayanna, who was married to John Phillips. Her two oldest sons were so tall that Alana didn't recognize them and their little girls were thriving. They also had to visit the Chicago eateries that anchored the Van-Buren restaurant family.

Alana was enjoying their getaway tremendously. His family was so warm and welcoming that she felt like she'd known them for years. His younger brother, Glenn, looked a lot like Roland, but he also favored his Creole father. He seemed to share his brother's taste in women because he looked at her with thoughtful eyes and said, "You have a younger sister that's single, don't you, Alana? I'm going to have to come visit Columbia really soon."

That sentiment was echoed by his sisters. They had decided to take her shopping at some of their favorite haunts, once they realized that she was an astute bargain hunter.

Roland was at VanBuren's, the flagship restaurant, when they decided to go to an outlet mall that boasted a Coach store and a shoe store with fabulous low prices. She was in the front seat and Marisa was driving when they stopped at a red light. Marisa gave her a sassy grin and asked if they'd started planning the wedding yet. Alana was about to tell her that Roland hadn't proposed when the light turned green and Marisa entered the intersection.

Suddenly there was a thunderous noise like nothing she'd ever heard before and then everything was dead still.

Alana woke slowly and in great pain. Her eyes didn't seem to work the first time; her lids were so heavy that they didn't want to lift so she rested for a moment and tried again. This time she got them all the way up and what she could see wasn't in any way familiar.

It was a completely strange room and when she tried to look around, she found that she couldn't turn her head. She tried to sit up and that didn't work, either. Finally, she heard a voice that she recognized.

"Hey, sweetheart, you're awake. Don't get scared, you and Marisa were in a little car accident and you're in the hospital. You're fine, she's fine and I'm here. I'm not leaving you for a minute, baby," Roland said softly.

She felt his hand grip hers and she smiled before drifting back to sleep. In a few hours she was awake again, but she was much more lucid this time. She could clearly see that Roland was there with a bandage on his forehead and a stunning black eye. To her utter shock, Aretha was there also, along with her father, Arthur, both of them looking concerned.

"Okay, is this some kind of weird theme party? What the heck is going on here? Mama and Daddy, when did you get to Chicago?" she asked. She licked her lips and frowned. "Can I have some water?"

Glendora came into her room then, followed by Renard. Roland poured her a cup of water from the little plastic pitcher on the tray table and she gamely sipped it through the bendy straw while more questions formed. Roland started talking while she sipped.

"Okay, baby, you remember when you and the girls were going shopping? Well, some ass came blazing through a red light and T-boned you. Your arm is broken, but you've already had surgery and it's going to be fine. You're a little bruised up from the airbags, but you're still gorgeous. Marisa was fine but her car is toast, which is nothing to worry about."

Alana nodded her head when he started talking but stopped when she realized that it made her head hurt, for one thing, and she still had on a very uncomfortable cervical collar, for another. "But what happened to you, baby? How did you get that black eye?" she asked Roland.

Aretha was happy to explain. "Sweetie, it was a hit-and-run," she explained. "When the police caught up with him they brought him to the emergency room because he was pretending to be hurt. He tried to escape and Roland caught him by the neck and beat him up," she said gleefully. "One of the policemen elbowed him when they tried to pull him off the idiot."

For some reason this struck Alana as being funny and she started to laugh, but that made her ribs hurt. After giving a proper greeting to her father and mother and Roland's parents, Alana realized something. "I need a mirror," she announced.

Aretha and Glendora exchanged glances and seemed to communicate silently. After what appeared to be a mental debate, they sighed and Aretha pulled out her Estée Lauder bronzer compact and handed it to Alana, who took a glimpse and yelped, handing it right back to her mother. She looked at Roland with a half smile.

"At least we match," she told him.

He managed a smile and leaned down to kiss her forehead. "Folks, can we have the room for a minute?" he asked.

The parents vanished as if by magic.

"Alana, I've never been so scared in my entire life. As soon as these black eyes heal, we're getting married. If anything was to happen to you I would lose my mind and that's the truth. If they hadn't pulled me off that little bastard I would've killed him for sure," he said.

"Roland, I'm so sorry I put you through this, I really am."

"Honey, it's not your fault, it's not Marisa's fault. That little bastard was high as a damned kite and texting while he drove.

It's all his fault. I love you so much that I can't even imagine my life without you. And Domino misses you, by the way. You should be able to come home tomorrow and she's going to be all over you."

Alana was sore and hungry, but nothing had ever looked better to her than Roland did right now. She pointed to her lower lip for a kiss. "This doesn't hurt, kiss me right here," she said.

"Darling, there's something else that I need to tell you," he said. "When you were in the emergency room and they were running blood tests and stuff to get you ready for surgery, the doctor found out something that you should know."

"Oh, yeah? Like what, I'm anemic or something?"

"No, honey, he found out that we're pregnant."

The next few days were like scenes from the sappiest rom-com ever conceived and Alana enjoyed every minute of it.

Once she got it through her head that she was truly carrying Roland's baby, she was content to bask in the collective love that surrounded her at his parents' home. She was so stunned by her test results that a specialist from the GYN department of

Stroger Hospital had to pay her a visit and explain. She was a petite Indian doctor who held her hand while delivering some extremely good news to Roland and Alana.

"Alana, I think your doctors were being overly cautious when they told you that a healthy, successful pregnancy might not be possible. You're going to want to consult your own physician when you go home to Columbia, but the preliminary testing that I did doesn't show anything in the way of scarring or any other kind of obstruction to a healthy baby. You're going to do just fine," she assured her. "You two are going to have a beautiful baby and I want you to come see me when you bring him or her to Chicago to visit."

After she left, Roland gave her a smile of pure happiness and teased, "Him, her or them, you never know in this family."

"I hope we have quadruplets in that case. Because you're going to be a very, very hands-on Dad, especially when it comes to diapers," she gloated.

"I'll be more than happy to," he said promptly. "Anything for my lovely one and our babies."

He was quite right about Domino missing her because when he carried her in the front door, Domino went crazy. She was on her hind legs doing pirouettes right out of *Swan Lake,* she was so glad to see her.

Glendora installed Alana in a guest room that had every comfort and she was never without company. Besides her mother and father and all of Roland's siblings, Jared's sisters, Tamara and Cam, came to visit and brought her a stack of books by Brenda Jackson, Janice Sims, Adrienne Byrd and Beverly Jenkins.

Emily and Ayanna also came, bringing their gorgeous mother, Lucie, who was laden down with brownies and tulips, and best of all, Damon and his children, Courtney and Gabriel, came, too.

"Auntie Alana, we made you a picture," Courtney told her. They each held a corner and proudly showed it off. They handed it to her and gave her sweet kisses before sitting down on the floor to play with Domino and Gwennie.

Gabriel had his own announcement for her.

"We're moving to South Carolina, Auntie Alana. We can see Sydney all the time and we're gonna have a puppy, too," he said excitedly. "I want a big one like Gwennie," he added as Gwennie gave him a sociable cheek snuffle.

"I want a little one like Domino," Courtney asserted.

"Damon, I'm so happy to hear that you're moving," Alana said. "Jared and Roland have been talking about putting new restaurants in Charleston, Myrtle Beach and Hilton Head for a long time now."

Damon, who was eerily identical to his twin, Lucas, nodded. "I really want the kids to be closer to Mom and Dad. They miss them something awful." His adopted twins were Afro-Asian; their late mother was black and their father was Chinese and they'd produced two adorable children. "Besides that, Columbia seems to be the place to be to find a wife," he joked. "My kids need a mom and if three bums like Jared, Lucas and Roland found beautiful brides in South Carolina there's hope for me yet," he said with a diabolical grin directed at Roland, who was coming through the door with refreshments.

"You know I'ma get you for that," Roland muttered as he struggled for balance when Domino dashed through his legs, followed by Gwennie and the twins. "You think you're funny, but you ain't." He put the tray down on a table by the window and turned to Damon, who was laughing at the jab he'd gotten in at Roland's expense.

"On second thought, I actually know a

really nice lady who'd be perfect for you. She's got a funny name, but other than that you two would hit it off great," he said with a suspiciously innocent look.

"Yeah? What's her name?" Damon asked.

"Shimmer. I'll hook you two up, you'll have a ball."

Damon left the room to round up his children while Alana reached for one of the fat chocolate chip cookies Roland had brought her. Before she could delve into the mystery of Shimmer, her father made an appearance.

"Hi, Daddy," she said, patting the side of the bed to indicate that he should sit down. "What's up?"

"Just came to check in with you. Your mother and I will be leaving tonight and I wanted to make sure that you have every-thing you need," he said after kissing her forehead and taking one of her cookies. Chocolate was a family weakness and he had no shame about getting his fair share.

"I'm so happy you guys came up to see about me. I still don't understand why you're driving back instead of flying," she said as she tried to get her cookie back.

"Look, I just do what I'm told," he said with a smile. "Life's much easier that way. So how are you feeling, Lana? Is there anything you need me to do?"

Alana lifted her right arm in its cast and indicated her position with the other. She was fully dressed except for shoes and other than her black eye and a few stitches on her forehead, she looked like herself. "Daddy, I am perfectly fine. I still have a little pain in my arm and my ribs, but I don't have a headache or anything. I'm lying on the bed because Mama and Glendora have been babying me so much, not to mention that my loving husband-to-be does everything for me except brush my teeth," she said happily. "There's not a thing in the world wrong except that a mean man took my cookie."

"You'll live," Arthur said dryly. He relented and gave her another one.

"Thank you, Daddy. Roland made these for me," she purred before taking her first bite. Roland was stretched out on the bed next to her, fiddling with his iPhone.

"Sweetheart, I have a feeling that there is very little that this man wouldn't do to make you happy. I'm going to lie down for a while before we hit the road. See you later," he said as he left the two of them alone.

"Roland, I'm so happy," she said. "I'm just so happy that I don't know if my heart can hold it all."

He captured her lips and licked the chocolate from the corner of her mouth. "You won't have to hold it all, honey. We're having a baby, remember? All that extra joy will come in handy in a few months."

She looked at him with wonder in her eyes. "We made a baby, Roland. We created a miracle, the two of us together," she said softly. "Our little miracle." She looked at her perfectly flat abdomen, trying to imagine what it was going to look like as the weeks went by.

"Umm, I hate to say I told you so, but if you recall, I told you that we made one. I knew the moment it happened," he said, popping his collar old-school style and giving her a sly wink.

"Conceited much? Are there any more cookies on that tray? And I need some milk, too, please."

Roland looked at her with his whole heart in his eyes. Her hair was messy, her eye was black-and-blue and she had a bandage on her forehead along with cookie crumbs on her cheeks and he knew he'd never see anyone more beautiful in his life. Nothing had prepared him for the strength of the love he felt for her but that was fine with him. Life with Alana was going to be a series of surprises, each one better than the next. He knew it as sure as he knew his own name. He had a couple of surprises for her, too, and he couldn't wait to see her light up with joy when she got them.

He didn't have to wait long for the first one. Alana insisted on coming downstairs for dinner with the family, saying it didn't make sense for her to be lounging around when she wasn't a bit sick. She only needed a bit of assistance getting in and out of the bathtub so that she didn't get her cast wet, and Roland was more than happy to help with that.

He also washed her back, a sweet but frustrating gesture because it was more arousing than hygienic. She didn't mind in the least; it felt so good.

She couldn't wait to get home so they could have as much noisy sex as possible, and she told him so, making him drop the sponge and get his pushed-up sleeve soaking wet in his effort to retrieve it.

"You need to give a man some warning when you're about to say something like that," he told her.

"Sorry, I wasn't thinking," she said demurely.

Sitting in the tub full of bubbles with her firm brown breasts with the lickable dark

228

nipples pointing at him, she was so desirable that he wanted to have that noisy unbridled sex right then and there, but he made himself stay strong.

With Marisa and Pamela's help, Alana looked pretty much like her normal self when she came downstairs. Marisa styled her hair in an attractive bun on top of her head and her bangs hid the bandage. Pamela applied her makeup and the mineral powder foundation she used covered her black eye nicely.

She wore a pair of violet wide-legged pants with a matching camisole and a fabulous Adrienne creation, a black jacket with kimono sleeves that was covered with exotic flowers.

Her future sisters-in-law were most impressed when she told them that the garment was made by her sister. They were equally excited about the annual sister swap and vowed to have one of their own. Pamela squealed when she saw the necklace and earrings from Roland.

"I'm going to have to rethink my dating program," she mumbled to herself. "I've obviously been doing something wrong all this time."

Alana was pleased to see Roland's eyes light up when she entered the living room.

Everyone had gathered there for pre-dinner drinks apparently, since everyone seemed to have a drink at hand. She looked around for Domino and Gwennie, but they were nowhere to be found. She turned to Roland to ask where they were, but he had his own agenda.

Taking her hand in his, he spoke to the room at large. "Everybody, I wanted this to be a special night for a lot of reasons. When I moved to Columbia, I had a lot of plans for the restaurant and my real estate port-folio and all that good stuff, but all my plans changed when I saw the beauty standing next to me. Everything changed in that one moment, even though I never believed in that kind of stuff, no matter what Jared and Lucas told me," he said, looking down at Alana. A ripple of laughter went through the room before he continued.

"But I can attest that when you meet your other half you know it. It can happen before you realize what's going on in your head or your heart. You just have to be smart enough to figure it out. I figured it out and now every dream I ever had is coming true. I had planned this a little differently, but I re-alized that time isn't promised to any of us, so . . ." He turned and gave a sharp whistle which brought Domino running with a bow around her neck. Attached to it was a small box, which he removed while Domino twirled around to applause and laughter.

He knelt in front of Alana, who had tears running down her face. "I had to have this delivered by special messenger because I wanted you to have it when I made this official. Alana, you are my everything. Nothing in my life has brought me as much happiness as the time I've spent with you and I never want it to end. I want you for a lifetime of lifetimes, Alana, starting with becoming my wife."

He slid a ring on her finger while all the women shed tears of happiness for the couple.

"Yes, Roland, I will. I thought I'd never have love again and you proved me wrong over and over again. I'm so happy that you love me because you're my heart and my soul and I can't wait for you to be my husband."

She looked at the ring for the first time and couldn't breathe for a moment. It was like nothing she'd ever seen before. It was so perfect that the tears started again. It was an oval cinnamon diamond of at least five carats, surrounded by three rows of fancy diamonds in chocolate, rose and pink and set in rose gold. It was obvious that he'd had it made just for her and it touched her heart so deeply that she fell in love with him all over again.

Domino danced around again as if she knew exactly what was going on and her happy barks signaled the beginning of a wonderful new life for the blissful couple. They were so involved in a deep, loving kiss that they didn't hear Pamela again telling Marisa that she was definitely going to change her dating criteria from here on out.

"If I can't have what they have, I don't want it," she sniffled. "Hand me a tissue, please."

CHAPTER 13

"I don't think there's a church in the state big enough to hold all these people," Aretha said with a sigh.

"You'll work it out, Mama, you always do," Alana said calmly.

They were in her living room working on wedding plans. That is, Aretha and Glendora were planning; Alana was holding her nephew, David Jared VanBuren III. She couldn't get enough of rubbing her cheek against his silky hair and inhaling his precious baby scent. At this stage in her pregnancy, her maternal instincts were raging and she absolutely doted on him.

Besides, she wasn't particularly interested in all the wedding plans. She just wanted to get married with no muss and no fuss but everyone vetoed that notion. Her parents were dead set against it because they'd missed her first wedding due to the hasty elopement.

Roland's parents wanted to see their oldest son get married in a nice ceremony since he was the first to marry. Sydney, Courtney and Gabriel wanted to be in the wedding and Roland's sisters did, too, so it was on and poppin'.

Alana agreed graciously, as long as someone else did the planning.

She was perfectly content to spend her time loving Roland and getting ready for their baby to come. Yes, it was going to be a barnyard-sized production with ten bridesmaids and an equal number of groomsmen, but it wasn't a problem for her.

She was more concerned with deciding who was going to manage Custom Classics, but even that wasn't a huge stumbling block because she was seriously considering selling the business. It was her idea; no one had tried to convince her that it was time to let it go, this was a conclusion she'd arrived at on her own. Roland was slightly astounded when she told him about it one morning while they were having breakfast.

He was completely supportive and agreed with her that divesting herself of the business was a practical plan. She'd had offers for the company before and now it was a matter of fielding the best one. She wanted to make sure that her employees were well taken care of and could keep their jobs because after all, it was their skill and creativity that had built the business into the profitable enterprise of which she was so proud.

Alexis was also on board with it because she was in the midst of making changes in her business life. After years of running two of the most successful salon/day spas in the state, Alexis was ready to hang up her curling irons for good.

"I don't know if I want to sell the business to Javier outright or just stay on as majority stockholder," she told Alana. "But I do know that I don't want to work there anymore. I want to stay home with my baby, for one thing, and for another, I want to start a food-related business. I want to start producing jams, jellies and preserves that are organic and healthy. I also want to make organic baby foods. Do you know what they put in the food that innocent babies are expected to consume?"

Alana made a face and said, "No, not really, it'll make me sick to think about it. Just get busy on it so our babies will never have to eat it."

The only person who wasn't walking around smiling and serene was Ava. It was an odd situation for her to be in, that was true. All three of her sisters were college graduates, highly successful and now they were reproducing while Ava was working as a receptionist in her sister's spa. It was a mercy job, at that. Alexis let her work there to give her something to do, basically.

Adrienne, who'd lived the farthest away for so long, had the most clarity about Ava's situation.

She told Alana as much when she was designing the dress in which Alana would be wed. "Something is really off with Ava and I think you all are too close to the situation to see it clearly. Ava was an A student all through high school and she was always on the dean's list at college. She has one semester between her and her bachelor's degree and for her to leave school, move home and while away her time means that something is going on, something serious."

Alana felt a wash of guilt as she listened to Adrienne. "You're right. We've all been so busy being self-righteous, self-involved and bossy that we haven't really helped our baby sister at all."

"We might not be the ones who can help her," Adrienne pointed out. "Maybe we need a more objective party to lend a listening ear."

"You're absolutely right, Adrienne, and

I'm really ashamed that I didn't see that much earlier. She's been acting out for a reason and we've been feeding into it instead of helping her handle it." Her eyes filled with tears and she looked around Adrienne's sewing room for a tissue.

"Hormone alert," Adrienne said cheerfully. "Go in the bathroom, don't wipe your nose on my fabric," she teased.

When Alana came back with a roll of toilet tissue, her ever-shifting hormones had gone back to normal. "Speaking of a listening ear, what did you and Royce Griffin talk about in terms of your situation? Was he helpful?"

Adrienne stuck her drawing pencil behind her ear and rubbed her burgeoning belly with her other hand. "He was very helpful," she admitted. "I'm still not worried about Sierra trying to swoop in and steal my baby because I haven't heard from her or her ex-husband. They seem to have forgotten that I was their surrogate and the baby inside me is theirs. So I've forgotten it, too. This is my baby and no one is going to stake a claim on him. I'd like to see them try it," she scoffed. "And by the way, that Royce Griffin is possibly the most gorgeous man I've ever seen in my life. Is he from another galaxy or something? Good Lord, the man is flawless," she said, shaking her head.

"Absolutely flawless and I should know because I've seen some of the best-looking men in Hollywood up close and personal." She laughed.

"Okay, this is what I have in mind for your dress. What do you think?" She held up her sketchpad for Alana's approval.

The tears started again as Alana saw the vision Adrienne had created. "It's perfect, the most beautiful thing I've ever seen. I love it. I love you," she sighed.

"I love you, too, Sissie. This is going to be the best wedding ever," she said. "With the most pregnant bridesmaids!"

In the end, it was a perfect wedding. Thanks to Aretha and Glendora's military precision in executing their plans, it went off without a flaw. They had managed to put together a formal wedding in record time and the ceremony took place on a beautiful August day.

Alana's dress was magnificent, made of pale green silk organza with an overlay of creamy guipure lace. It was off-the-shoulder with a sweetheart neckline that showed off her sculpted collarbones and the delicate line of her neck. Her hair was worn up accented with real gardenias and she looked like a Thomas Blackshear figurine.

She and Roland had decided to have a "first look," a new tradition in which the bride and groom saw each other before the ceremony.

Roland waited for her in a secluded part of the botanical garden where they were having the outdoor ceremony. He didn't hear her approaching, so when she touched his back and he turned around, it was a magical moment. She was carrying her bouquet of purple, green and white tulips, calla lilies and gardenias and he was momentarily struck dumb by her beauty. They simply stared at each other, drinking in the sight of their soul's mate. Roland looked just as handsome as she was beautiful, wearing an ivory shirt and slacks with a pale green vest.

"I can't wait to get you alone," he said softly. "I can't believe that you're mine for a lifetime."

"We're yours," she said, putting his hand on her still-small belly. "We're yours now and forever."

The wedding party was huge but exceptionally gorgeous. Adrienne was her maid of honor and Alexis was the matron of honor. Ava, Sherri, Tollie, and all five of Roland's sisters were the bridesmaids, all in pale green.

Jared was the best man, with Lucas, Damon, Duncan, Royce and a bunch of Roland's handsome friends and cousins as the groomsmen.

Sydney, Courtney and Gabriel were the flower girls and ring bearer, and Domino was also in attendance, trotting happily down the aisle with Gabriel. She had on a big lavender bow and she knew she was the star of the procession.

Everything went beautifully with one small hitch; after they were pronounced man and wife, Alana and Roland couldn't seem to stop kissing. No one minded in the least, though.

The reception was as wonderful as the wedding. It was held at Seven-Seventeen, which by now was considered a lucky place for receptions. That's where Alexis and Sherri had had theirs and Alana saw no reason on earth to break with tradition.

The food was superb, the ambiance was romantic and their pets were treated like honored guests.

Somehow, amidst all the celebrating, Roland and Alana managed to get away from everyone.

The back of Seven-Seventeen was a big garden area with a deck and outdoor tables. Down the path through the garden was a gazebo and to Alana's surprise, there was a bottle of non-alcoholic passion fruit spumante, two flutes and under glass was one of Alana's favorite things in the world, caviar and toast points.

"This was a brilliant idea, Roland," she said as their glasses touched.

"I'm full of brilliant ideas, honey, especially when it comes to you and me. I had a flash of real genius the day I met you and that's what gave me the brilliant idea that I would do anything on this earth to make you mine. Now I'll do whatever it takes to keep you as happy as you are now for the rest of our lives. You're my heart, Alana. You're my life from now on."

He kissed her tenderly and used her handkerchief to dab away her tears. She kissed him back and said, "And you are mine, now and forever. I want to stay here all night," she whispered.

"That sounds romantic but our mamas would have our heads. Let's go in, honey. We have forever together."

She smiled up at him and agreed. "Yes, we do."

ABOUT THE AUTHOR

Melanie Schuster started reading when she was four and believes that's why she's a writer today. She was always fascinated with books and loved telling stories. From the time she was very small she wanted to be a writer. She fell in love with romances when she began reading the ones her mother would bring home. She would go to any store that sold paperbacks and load up! When she had a spare moment she was reading. Schuster loves romance because it's always so hopeful. Despite the harsh realities of life, romance always brings to mind the wonderful, exciting adventure of falling in love and meeting your soul mate. She believes in love and romance with all her heart. She finds fulfillment in writing stories about compelling couples who find true, lasting love in the face of all the obstacles out there. She hopes all of her readers find their true love. If they've already been lucky enough to find love, she hopes that they never forget what it felt like to fall in love.